Buenos Aires Docs

Finding the prescription for a love that lasts...

Meet the dedicated medics of the
Hospital General de Buenos Aires. They might be
winners in their work, but they all need a little help
when it comes to finding their happy-ever-afters!

Luckily for them, passion is sweeping through the
corridors of the hospital like a virus and no one
is immune! Are they brave enough to take their
chance on happiness...and each other?

Find out in

Sebastián and Isabella's story
ER Doc's Miracle Triplets by Tina Beckett

Carlos and Sofia's story
Surgeon's Brooding Brazilian Rival by Luana DaRosa

Gabriel and Ana's story
Daring to Fall for the Single Dad by Becky Wicks

Felipe and Emilia's story
Secretly Dating the Baby Doc by JC Harroway

All available now!

T0112836

Dear Reader,

What a thrill it was to be able to team up with a group of three other Harlequin Medical Romance authors and put these four Buenos Aires Docs books together. It felt like we created our own little world, where magic happened daily, not just on the pages for our characters, but in the emails we shared, discussing our stories.

I can't wait to work with more of them again. In fact, Luana and I are working on a Valentine's Day duet as we speak!

I really hope you enjoy this dalliance in the dazzling city of Buenos Aires, where my hero Gabriel has his work cut out as a single dad, and that's *before* his childhood trailblazer friend Ana shows up in his life again. Will a long-term crush turn into more as Ana launches a new, hectic family clinic, or will the past come back to bite them? Read on to find out.

Becky x

DARING TO FALL FOR THE SINGLE DAD

BECKY WICKS

MEDICAL ROMANCE

Special thanks and acknowledgment are given to Becky Wicks for her contribution to the Buenos Aires Docs miniseries.

Harlequin®
MEDICAL
ROMANCE

ISBN-13: 978-1-335-94244-9

Daring to Fall for the Single Dad

Copyright © 2024 by Harlequin Enterprises ULC

Harlequin Enterprises ULC
22 Adelaide St. West, 41st Floor
Toronto, Ontario M5H 4E3, Canada
www.Harlequin.com

Printed in U.S.A.

Born in the UK, **Becky Wicks** has suffered interminable wanderlust from an early age. She's lived and worked all over the world, from London to Dubai, Sydney, Bali, New York City and Amsterdam. She's written for the likes of *GQ*, *Hello!*, *Fabulous* and *Time Out*, and has written a host of YA romance, plus three travel memoirs—*Burqalicious*, *Balilicious* and *Latinalicious* (HarperCollins, Australia). Now she blends travel with romance for Harlequin and loves every minute! Tweet her @bex_wicks and subscribe at beckywicks.com.

Books by Becky Wicks

Harlequin Medical Romance

From Doctor to Daddy
Enticed by Her Island Billionaire
Falling Again for the Animal Whisperer
Fling with the Children's Heart Doctor
White Christmas with Her Millionaire Doc
A Princess in Naples
The Vet's Escape to Paradise
Highland Fling with Her Best Friend
South African Escape to Heal Her
Finding Forever with the Single Dad
Melting the Surgeon's Heart
A Marriage Healed in Hawaii

Visit the Author Profile page
at Harlequin.com for more titles.

To my lovely dad, Ray Wicks, who is definitely not single and will probably never read this. You'll always be my number one anyway.

CHAPTER ONE

HOLDING UP A HAND, Dr Ana Mendez waved at the post boy, smiling at his pink feathered headdress as he zoomed past her windows on his bicycle.

'I guess everyone's getting in the spirit already,' she said to her vase of fresh marigolds. It was early now, and relatively peaceful on the streets, but in just a few hours her city would be pumping with a thousand kinds of music, dancing groups and musicians in every side street. The crowds would be shuffling in colourful costumes through the blocks and barrios, and her ears would be assaulted from all angles as every speaker tried its best to compete with the rest. The first day of Carnival was always fun in Buenos Aires—*unless you worked in A&E*, she thought to herself. The staff at the hospital were always run off their feet at this time of year. Luckily this clinic wasn't opening till Monday, so she had the perfect excuse to hide away from the mayhem.

Ah, this clinic—*her* new clinic! Steering her wheelchair expertly to the desk, breathing in the smell of the fresh paint, Ana glanced at the plaque on the wall above her MD certificate. Her lips twitched with a proud smile at the sight of her name glistening in silver: Dr Ana Mendez. She had her own practice…finally!

She and her small but excited team had decided to get the madness of Carnival over with first, but every day had dawned with a new set of tasks to complete in the run up to opening. She'd been coming here every day with new additions in preparation, or to assist the workmen with new equipment, new lighting or new posters. Any excuse would do, because this was all so exciting. So…not what people had expected someone like her to go and do.

Turning her chair back towards her consulting room, she noted how at home the snake plant she'd brought in today looked already. 'Very nice, *mijo*, I think this place is ideal for you,' she said to it. Its sword-like leaves with bold stripy patterns suited the corner of her desk, she decided, and, best of all, it could survive with little help— just like her.

After years of working her way up and around hospitals all over Argentina, she had finally taken over the barrio's clinic round the corner from the home she'd grown up in, and moved into her new wheelchair-adapted apartment too. Dr Azaban, the old GP, had hung up her coat and retired just a few months ago. The call had come in while Ana was on a break from a shift at the Medical Medicina Privada in Bariloche, where she'd been for the best part of five years.

'The time is now, Ana,' she'd said, in the phone call that would change the direction of her life. 'Are you ready to come home and take over?'

It had taken a while, a lot of prep, a lot of money and a lot of documentation but she'd sailed through it all with one goal on the horizon—a home from home, a place to call hers and a new, refreshed clinic for the community to call theirs. She'd always said, when she came home, it would be for something worthwhile. Dr Azaban was an old family friend who'd been preparing Ana for this since she'd completed her studies. Not that it wasn't going to take a while to readjust—she was still bumping into people she'd forgotten to tell she was even back in Recoleta!

Ana adjusted a bright-red truck on the colourful mat in the children's section of the waiting room, then sat up straighter a soft blue teddy bear on his tiny stool. It had been decided years ago, and even laid out on her vision board, that *her* clinic would possess none of the drabness she'd encountered in other GP practices over the years. The process of getting well began in the mind, in cheery surroundings with positive vibes, she reminded herself, plucking a colourful marigold from another vase on the magazine stand and placing it behind her ear.

This was something she'd taken on board as a child, when the kind staff at the children's ward at Hospital General de Buenos Aires had sat her down and explained how she would likely never walk again. At just six years old, she'd lain there after the car accident, wondering how on earth she'd get by without the use of her legs. She'd been too young to fathom how hard it would be, not just on her going forward but also on her parents, Juan and Martina. She'd been too young to understand anything then, except the kindness and good intentions of the people around her and the way the bright colours had made her feel.

In those dark times she'd grown to find a sense of hope in the cheery flowers and toys, the pretty fabrics of the blankets and the reassuring faces on the posters on the walls. Everything ever since had been about colour, she thought now, catching a glimpse of herself in the window. She didn't need Carnival as an excuse to dress up as though she'd wheeled her chair through a rainbow and come out draped in it on the other side. Her bright-yellow polka-dot headscarf held back her long mass of raven black curls and matched her shoes. She always matched her headscarves to her shoes wherever possible.

A banging on the door made her start. 'We're

not open yet!' she called. But the banging continued, this time louder. *What the…?*

Ana sped for the door, only to find a white-haired man doubled over on the pavement, clutching his chest. 'Mr Acosta!' she cried, recognising in shock the seventy-something man from the shop over the road.

'I think I'm having a heart attack, Ana,' he managed, his face creased in pain. No soon had she flung open the doors than he was lurching forward, practically landing on her lap in the wheelchair.

'Come in, we'll get you help!' Her words were reassuring, even as she swiftly lowered her chair as far down as it would go. Bundling him inside across the threshold onto the cool floor, she loosened his collar with one hand and called for an ambulance with the other, praying the streets weren't yet too packed with Carnival revellers for it to reach them. Pressing an ear to his chest, the rhythm of his heart was evident, which would buy some time, but she carefully tilted back his head on the tiles, keeping his airways clear. 'You're going to be OK, Mr Acosta.'

Thankfully, the sound of a siren in the distance soon gave her comfort, and within minutes she was watching two men leap expertly from the vehicle outside, Ambu bags bouncing on their hips. Then she realised who was wearing the first paramedic's uniform.

Oh, my God.

'Gabriel Romero,' she mouthed in surprise as the world stopped.

He pulled up short in front of her. 'Ana?'

Her old friend looked at her wide-eyed, and she took in the full extent of his dashing looks in a fraction of a second: the piercing yet warm brown eyes that had steadied her as a child and teenager into adulthood; the thick chocolate-brown hair that matched his beautiful dark skin; his sculpted face; and those adorable dimples that had always made him seem more boy than man. Now at thirty-two, as was she, he was just all man. Their locked gaze left her breathless, before any surprise at seeing him was quickly overshadowed by the severity of Mr Acosta's condition.

His partner, Bruno Gomez—whom admittedly she hadn't known as well as Gabriel had over the years—dropped to his knees beside the man. He swiftly assessed the situation. 'Pulse is weak, respirations are shallow,' he murmured to Gabriel, his gloved hand checking for signs of life. Mr Acosta wasn't moving now and dread pooled in her stomach.

Gabriel looked up. 'Possible myocardial infarction. Get the AED ready, Bruno.'

Bruno nodded and reached for the automated

external defibrillator from their medical bag. 'AED's ready, Gabe.'

Bruno attached the AED pads to Mr Acosta's chest as Gabriel continued monitoring his vital signs. 'Analysing,' the AED's automated voice announced. They both stepped back as it assessed the situation. Ana held her breath. 'Shock advised. Stand clear.'

A surge of anxiety gripped her, and she fought to stop herself gripping Gabriel's arm. She had seen her share of medical emergencies, of course, but the urgency of this moment in her as yet unopened clinic seemed different for some reason. She glanced at Gabriel, who nodded, his face determined.

'Clear,' he declared as the AED administered the shock. The man's body jolted briefly as the electric current coursed through him.

Bruno leaned in, listening to the man's chest with a stethoscope. The man's face made her want to cry suddenly. No! She could not have a man die here, not now, not ever! Her clinic would be a big failure before it even launched, and as for poor Mr Acosta...

'We've got him!' came Gabriel's relieved announcement. 'OK, we're good, let's get him to hospital.'

The two men talked coolly and calmly to Mr Acosta, and fixed him with the breathing apparatus. Ana remained calm and collected, making a call to Mr Acosta's wife to tell her what was happening.

At the same time, she couldn't help the way her mind was reeling, not just with the adrenaline of the moment, but with the rapid-fire memories coming at her the more she watched Gabriel in action. He had done a lot to help bring her to this point… Actually, did he even know this was now her clinic? He had always wanted more for her. He was the one who'd encouraged her to apply for medical school in the first place!

In minutes, they had Mr Acosta on the stretcher, breathing heavily but stable. Ana held the door open for the two paramedics, and grabbed her own car keys.

'I'll follow you,' she said on the street, motioning to her wheelchair-adapted vehicle outside.

'Are you sure? It's getting pretty crazy out here already.' Gabriel held her eyes for a second over the stretcher as he heaved it up into the back of the ambulance with Bruno. Her breath caught in her throat as he leaned out through the doorway, reached for her face and adjusted something in her hair. She had clean forgotten the marigold was still there, sticking out from behind her ear.

'They were always your favourite flowers,' he said, just before Bruno called to him, offering her an apologetic look over Gabriel's shoulder. Ana fought the flush warming her cheeks.

'I'll meet you in A&E,' she said quickly, sweeping past him, surprised and marginally annoyed by the fluttering in her belly at a time when she could have done with staying calm.

As she drove behind the ambulance in the blare of its siren, her cheek tingled with the lingering feeling of him rearranging flower in her hair after all this time. Of course, the city was big, but the medical scene was small, so it had always been just a matter of time before their paths crossed again.

Still, now she couldn't stop thinking about their history together. Five years was a long time to go without seeing her friend, maybe even too long to pick up where they'd left off without it being a little weird, she thought, taking in a crowd of teens in feathers and sequins drinking soda by a pulsating speaker. Ana being in Bariloche for the last five years had cemented the divide, but they'd fallen out of touch even before that. She supposed he'd been too busy to check in as much, just as she had. He was a dad now; Dads were always busy. Or maybe those were just the excuses she'd been telling herself to trick her mind into falling out of love with him…

'Mr Acosta is going to be fine; he's stable, and his wife is on her way,' Gabriel said later, closing the door to the treatment room and motioning Ana to accompany him down the hall. 'Coffee?'

With the elderly man settled in recovery, Ana thought, what was another thirty minutes? Especially if it meant finding out what Gabriel Romero had been up to all this time.

Her heartbeat intensified yet again as she motored her chair alongside him through the labyrinth of corridors. Silly, she scorned herself. Once, maybe years ago, she'd had a hard crush on Gabriel, but that had been stomped out pretty fast once she'd realised he definitely did not feel the same way about her. The fact that he'd had a child with a relative stranger proved she'd hardly known him at all, really!

He looks beyond handsome in his uniform, though, she thought to herself as they made for the cafeteria. And Ana didn't miss the way he kept shooting her sideways glances as he stopped briefly to discuss something with a tall, muscular man whose name tag read 'Dr Carlos Cabrera'. She'd never seen Carlos before.

A&E was a hubbub of activity as usual. Nurses called out names, another ambulance arrived in a blare of sirens outside and Ana wheeled her chair alongside Gabriel, noting the acrid, astringent smell in the air and the lack of colour. Her clinic would always smell fresh, if she could help it, such as using flowers, she decided. It would always be a place of calm…at least, compared to this. It was more than a little strange just being here in the giant, hectic Hospital General de Buenos Aires, after all the time she'd spent in quieter, smaller establishments, let alone being with Gabriel.

'You look really well,' Gabriel said, holding open the cafeteria door for her. 'I see you're still as colourful as I remember. Nice shoes, by the way.'

'Why, thank you!' He was such a charmer. That hadn't changed, then. Gabriel had always complimented her choice of clothing, unlike her mother, who'd suggested on more than one occasion that it was unprofessional. Ana disagreed, of course. Mama was always trying to help in ways Ana didn't need her to; besides, she could do her job in any size, shape or colour of clothing, as long as she was always sitting down. Not everyone knew how to approach a GP in a wheelchair, so she'd learned over the years to hit them with the real her before they could imagine her as someone else in their own heads.

Gabriel sat her down in a quiet corner of the cafeteria, undisturbed. Soon they were sipping their coffees. His dark hair was still short, almost shaved to the scalp, which only intensified his liquid brown eyes as they talked.

Her stomach twisted with guilt as he talked

about Javi. The little boy was already five—how had that even happened? Maybe he thought she was a terrible friend for not reaching out sooner... but he'd have been so busy, being a father to baby Javi, and she'd felt bad taking up his time. He had always wanted to be there for her, so maybe a part of her had felt that, if she wasn't around, he wouldn't be able to and she'd free him somehow. The distance had also been a pretty convenient way to get over her unrequited crush, seeing as never in a million years would he feel the same way about her.

'How are your parents? I see Martina quite a lot in the grocery store; she always says you take ages to return her calls.' He grinned even as Ana flinched.

'Well, now, my mother can just walk down the street to me, like old times,' she said with a wry smile. 'Lucky me.'

He stifled a laugh and she felt her eye twitch. Gabriel knew how overbearing both Juan and Martina had always been. She'd been lucky, she supposed. Well, as lucky as a girl with a spinal cord injury could be, in that she'd never let other people's impressions of her, or her condition, stand in her way. Not that people hadn't tried. Her own parents, as well-meaning as they were, had never abandoned their tendency to try and wrap her up safe and tight in cotton wool. There'd

been a decade when they'd barely let her leave
the house alone. She'd had to battle every cousin,
aunt, uncle and grandparent over the years to be
able to do anything independently at all.

But Gabriel…he'd always been different.
Consequently, her crush on him had grown and
grown, until she'd almost been bursting with her
secret feelings. Gabriel had been the ever-present
friend, platonic, and completely oblivious to the
fact that, upon reaching their teenage years, and
with the two of them being pretty much insepa-
rable, Ana had wanted more.

The cafeteria was filled with people, and the
sound of voices talking filled the air, along with
the strong smell of coffee. It should have been
quite comfortable talking to him, despite her
old feelings, which had probably started around
the time she'd turned twelve or thirteen. They'd
grown up together after all, the two of them and
their families. He'd been the first one to jump in
front of her whenever one of the mean kids had
tried to bully her because of her wheelchair—
her hero! But he'd never known about her massive crush on him. How could he? She'd feared
his rejection so much that she'd never told him.
And, besides, how could she tell him that, hear
him say, 'Er, no thanks, Ana' and *then* go back
to being friends? There was just no way!

There had been one point when he'd asked to

see her, all serious and nervous-looking, and she'd freaked out inside, thinking, finally, he was going to tell her he *knew* how she felt about him, and that he had feelings for her too. Her heart had swelled to the size of a balloon as she'd sat there opposite him in the park, watching him wringing his hands together.

Just kiss me, she'd willed him. *Just do it before I burst!*

Then of course he'd told her about Ines being pregnant and that they were going to make it work because she wanted to keep the baby. Talk about being blindsided.

'So…tell me about this clinic,' he said now, gesturing with his cup. 'I saw the plaque on the wall, Ana. I know it's what you always wanted. Look at you, taking over from the barrio's favourite GP. Dr Az only ever had you in mind for that. When does it reopen?'

Ana breathed a harried sigh through her lips. 'I know, crazy, right? It opens officially on Monday.' She told him how she'd been so worried that things wouldn't come together in time, but soon her usual excitement was shining through as she told him all about her plans—from hiring the staff and finding donations from local businesses for the toys and furnishings, to decorating the interior and selecting medical equipment—it felt as if no detail was too small for her to go into. He listened intently, as he always did.

'It all sounds very impressive.' He smiled warmly. There were those butterflies again, she thought. They flapped even harder in her chest as he added softly, 'You were missed around here, you know.'

She flushed again, readjusting her yellow headscarf. 'By who, your mother? How is she?'

Gabriel laughed softly. 'She's well.'

Ana looked away for a moment, suddenly not sure what to say all over again. 'It must have been different in Bariloche,' he continued into the awkward silence that had just descended. 'Wasn't it cold in the foothills of the Andes?'

'Sometimes, but I loved my work, and that's where I spent most of my time. It was a pretty small clinic, not unlike the one I'm opening.'

Gabriel eyes narrowed indecipherably as he studied her, and he sat back in his seat. 'But you took yourself somewhere different; you embraced the challenge. I'm proud of you, Ana.'

Ana bit her lip, wishing the stupid butterflies would calm down—this was Gabriel, her friend! 'You helped give me the courage, remember? You cheered me on.'

'Maybe so, but you still would have done it without me. You always just did everything you set your mind to. You've seen so much more than I ever will. You've travelled…'

'You can still travel,' she told him, noticing the flecks of gold around his pupils that she'd always thought made his eyes look like marigolds shimmering in deep, dark pools. For so long, she'd been living life on her own—away from family and old friends—so it was kind of hard to fathom how anyone wouldn't want that experience, even if it wasn't for long. A few years, or even months away, doing things by oneself, and *for* oneself, could do wonders for the self-esteem.

'I can't go far, can I? I have my family, Javi and his dog…'

'Oh, I know!' She nodded, realising how naive and idealistic she must sound. Fathers of five-year-old kids didn't just uproot themselves and go work on the other side of the country.

'How is Javi liking school?' she asked now. 'I assume you share custody with Ines?'

In that moment, something seemed to shift between them. Gabriel pressed his palms together.

'Things are a little different now, yes,' he said quietly. The tension was rising by the second. He hunched his shoulders suddenly, gripping his coffee cup so hard it looked about ready to break. Surely he wasn't still upset about the separation with Ines? Ana knew they'd tried hard to make it work for the sake of the baby, but the baby had been the result of a quick fling over five *years* ago!

Ana was just about to ask what was wrong when someone called his name. They turned to see a heavily pregnant medic hurrying over to them as best she could, scraping back chairs to fit herself and her belly through, muttering apologies to people as she moved.

'There you are.' Ana studied her name badge: Dr Isabella Lopez. Isabella blew a long, shiny black curl from her face as she stopped in front of them, squinting her dark eyes a moment. Gabriel shot up and helped her into a chair, and she pressed two hands to her belly. 'Sorry guys; hi.' She huffed, introducing herself quickly to Ana. 'I'm glad I caught you, Gabe, I have a huge favour to ask you.'

Gabriel nodded in understanding as Isabella explained how she wasn't feeling very well, how her pregnancy was doing a number on her sleep patterns and that she didn't think she could handle the medical post at Carnival tonight. She was expecting triplets!

'I'm so sorry to ask at such short notice,' she said now, her tired brown eyes pleading. Isabella pressed a hand over his and rubbed another over her sweating forehead in a way that made Ana wonder what on earth it must feel like, having a tiny human inhabiting you, let alone three of them

throwing your internal systems all out of whack.
She had parts that didn't work as they should herself, namely her legs, but being pregnant must be
something else entirely.

'No need to apologise, Bella. Of course I'll
cover for you; you go home and rest,' Gabriel said
kindly. Ana realised she was staring at him over
the table now, and that her heart was melting at
his kindness. And Isabella was looking between
them with some interest.

'My parents are taking Javi tonight anyway;
they'll probably take his dog too, seeing as they
adore him,' Gabriel added, glancing at Ana, as if
knowing full well she'd ask, *what dog?* 'Actually,
they might leave the dog behind. Carnival is no
place for canines. He's a rescue dog called Savio,
a terrier mix—super-smart. He lives with Ines
and Pedro but we're teaching him tricks when he
visits. Pedro—that's Ines's new husband—picked
him up from a farm. Savio killed a chicken, so
they were about to put him to sleep for it, but the
poor thing was starving. They hadn't fed him in
a week, can you believe that?'

Ana's mouth had fallen open, but not just because of the chicken-killing dog and his troubled
life on the farm. Ines had remarried; when on
earth had that happened? Usually she got all the
gossip from her mother. Maybe she *should* have
returned more of Mama's calls.

OK, so there was a lot she didn't know about Gabriel's life these days, she mused despondently. Before she had even thought about what the heck she was doing, she turned to Isabella.

'I can help him this evening.' She smiled broadly. 'If that's OK?'

'Really?' Gabriel looked surprised and the fluttering started back up in Ana's stomach lining. 'You have so much to do before the clinic's opening; you should take tonight to relax!'

Isabella reached out and took Ana's hand in her own slightly clammy one, squeezing it gently before letting go. 'You're opening a clinic?'

Ana answered all of the sweet Isabella's questions, feeling Gabriel's eyes on her face the whole time. She wasn't quite sure, as later she made her way back out to her car, whether it was the clinic's impending opening that kept the butterflies soaring around her internal pathways or the thought of having Gabriel back in her world after all this time.

CHAPTER TWO

THE CROWDS THRONGED and bulged in the boulevards beyond their makeshift medical tent, and the music threatened to deafen Ana as she welcomed in a teenage boy.

'I think I sprained my wrist.' He winced at them as Gabriel pulled out a chair, his name tag swinging from his uniform top. The boy's face was ghostly white against his neon-yellow headdress as Gabriel ushered him into the chair and dropped to his haunches in front of him.

Meanwhile, someone else stuck in their head. Ana kindly asked the woman, who looked to be in her late thirties, to take another seat, reminding her to bend down first, so her peacock hat with all its turquoise feathers wouldn't break against the canvas ceiling. 'I'll be with you soon,' she said, noting her grazed knees. Maybe she'd fallen off her stilts.

'It's getting crazier by the minute,' Gabriel whispered as he hurried past Ana's wheelchair for more gauze. In the three hours since they'd set up in the medical tent, they'd already tended to three cases of fainting, thanks to the suffocating crowds; one food poisoning, thanks to endless empanadas and other fried snacks that had been left out in the sun all day; and even an elderly lady in her eighties who'd tripped on some steps in her high heels.

Still, Ana thought, glancing at Gabriel with the teenage boy, she probably wouldn't want to be here with anyone else. If she hadn't been working here, she'd have been hiding out at home, prepping for the clinic's opening on Monday, as if she wasn't ready by now—the last time she'd been in, it had been to tend to her snake plant, for goodness' sake. Although, it was lucky she had, otherwise what would have happened to poor Mr Acosta?

She wouldn't have been reunited with Gabriel, and she wouldn't be here now, checking out his cute butt in his uniform trousers every chance she got. It wasn't as if the carnival got her pumped as it did most people in Buenos Aires, even though she'd missed a few while working away from big cities. Her wheelchair wasn't best suited for squeezing through crowds.

'Remember that time you got stuck out there on Pinamar beach?' Gabriel said later when they finally found themselves with a moment to themselves. They were standing in the doorway to the tent, watching a kaleidoscope of colourful crimson tailored suits shimmy past, the men's fedoras tilted at rakish angles under the twilight sky.

'How could I forget?' Ana grimaced as a marching band of women followed, shimmering in sequinned dresses like gems. In fact, she was blushing now, just thinking about how she'd called everyone in their friendship group for help, and only Gabriel had been paying enough attention in the height of Carnival's chaos to realise she was missing and to answer. They'd gone as a group to the *balneários* and rented a wheelchair-friendly apartment, at Gabriel's insistence.

'You came to get me.' She smiled to herself, and he grinned, nodding slowly.

'I got you out of that sand pile and away from those drunks pretty fast. They were determined to dress you and your chair up in the Brazilian flag.'

Ana bit back a smile. 'My hero,' she said, remembering how she'd been on the verge of a panic attack when he'd raced across the sand and rescued her. He'd given the guys a massive telling off, then had forced them to apologise, which they had done sheepishly.

'Ines wasn't impressed. We were gone for hours, remember?' he said. Ana's stomach dropped like a sack of lead. Of course, he'd been trying to get back to Ines. She'd been pregnant then, and Ana had been trying her best to keep him to herself whilst simultaneously trying to get over her crush on him. It hadn't helped either cause to have him rushing off the minute Ines had called with another demand.

Just then, they were forced apart in the doorway by the arrival of a young man in a green hat covered in purple balloons. He limped towards them and proceeded to drop to his haunches at Gabriel's feet.

'I ran out of water; can you help me?' he slurred at them, and a balloon popped on his chest as he made to grab for Ana's knees. Gabriel held him back as she steered herself away quickly for the oxygen and some water.

'What are you supposed to be?' she heard Gabriel ask the guy.

'Sour grapes.' The man grunted. Despite himself and his drunken situation, he laughed. Ana bit back a smile and saw Gabriel do the same as the human sour grapes gulped down the water and breathed a sigh of relief so hard, she thought the tent might blow over.

Gosh, Gabriel's smile. He'd always lit up every room with that. His family adored him, and he them. In fact, they were the reason he'd said he'd never go anywhere else, even before he'd become a dad. The Romeros had never been the wealthiest family in the neighbourhood, but they'd never been lacking in love for each other. He was so good to them, just as now he was probably so good to his son Javi. He looked incredibly handsome in his uniform, too. And his cheekbones…

Ana had to look away before he caught her staring again. She just hadn't seen him in a while, and her old self was still acting on autopilot around him, that was all. The mild crush she'd had on him was all water under the bridge; thank heavens he'd never had a clue! But she could see the impression he made on everyone who came in here. His warmth radiated and instantly made everything better.

'You know,' she said, raising her voice above the blaring music from the passing parade, 'You're pretty good at all this. Maybe I should be hiring you to work for me at the clinic!'

Gabriel smirked, and suddenly Ana was flooded by paranoia. Shoot, she shouldn't have said that. Had that sounded as if she wanted him there with her? As if she needed him? That was the last impression she wanted to give him. He'd spent enough of his childhood, and his adult life, coming to her rescue.

As the hours went on and the patients rolled in, Ana found herself thinking more and more about that day at the beach—how they'd piled into a friend's giant van and driven the four hours south, laughing the whole way—well, the others had been laughing. She'd been trying to keep the scowl off her face at the way Ines had kept raking her long fingers through Gabriel's hair in the seat in front of hers. The job in Bariloche had been on the horizon then, but she hadn't told anyone yet. In truth, she'd wanted to tell Gabriel first, maybe just to gauge his reaction. He had been her champion, of course, and had told her to go for it. So, bolstered by the fact that she'd already lost him, and feeling as though she'd only be getting in the way if she stayed, she'd gone for it.

They'd drifted apart after that. The baby had arrived. The texts and emails had dried up. Looking at him now, she couldn't help wondering about his life now. They hadn't really gone into it too much beyond work stuff…and maybe she'd talked more than him, no thanks to her nerves. He was a single dad, and she assumed was living alone, seeing as he hadn't mentioned having a partner. And Ines had a new husband. The questions had been hovering on her tongue all day but the timing had just never felt right. Well, that and the fact that between them they could barely finish a sentence before someone blasted reggae, drum and bass or yelled over a microphone right outside the tent.

Finally, their tent was clear again. She wheeled back to the doorway, but Gabriel seemed glued to his phone now. Maybe he was chatting to a date, she thought idly, surprised at the pinpricks of jealousy that rose on the back of her neck. It had been weird enough when he'd admitted he'd had slept with Ines, let alone that he'd got her pregnant. Funny how she'd always kind of thought of him as hers.

'Check him out,' Gabriel said, walking over to her and handing her his phone. 'Doesn't he look great in that costume? I helped him pick it out at the fancy dress shop.'

Ana studied the photo of Javier. He was dressed as a ladybird in a bright-red fuzzy suit with huge black polka dots. He was so cute it almost hurt her eyes, and he was the spitting image of Gabriel when he'd been that age.

'Where are they?' she asked.

'Out and about somewhere. My parents would have taken him to all the kids' stuff. There's a children's parade soon; it'll be his first time taking part in it.'

'And you're missing it; that's a shame,' Ana said before she could think. A look of mild remorse fell across his handsome face, just as four people brushed past them, twirling around each other in some version of a tango, and almost sent them flying into each other. Gabriel caught her chair from behind and twirled her himself. Then he danced with her a moment on the pavement outside the tent, making her laugh as she spun her chair round and round. A group of women in antlers waving glow sticks stopped to cheer and whoop.

Gabriel used to do that a lot, back when she'd been feeling sorry for herself at being stuck in the stupid chair. Most of the time she'd been the picture of strength and determination... Well, that was what other people had seen. Gabriel had always known better. He'd seemed to instinctively know whenever she'd needed a reminder that she could do anything she put her mind to.

'You're still an excellent dancer, *chica*,' he told her, and she rolled her eyes, not quite managing to hide her laugh as one of the women removed her glittery antlers and placed them on his head. Gabriel went along with this new deer headpiece, performing another twirl to rapturous applause. He looked so ridiculous, she thought, smiling. Why would those butterflies not go away?

Gabriel was just doing a few quick steps of his own strange tango in front of her, making her laugh more and more with every exaggerated move, when another message came in on his phone. Soon, the headpiece and the onlookers were gone, and he was showing her a video. This time Javier was waving at him between his grandparents, whom she recognised, of course. Gabriel's ever-enthusiastic, ever the life of the party, parents were wearing matching bumble bee outfits, looking the epitome of the perfect grandparents.

'Hi, Papa!' Javier called out to the camera.

A jolt struck Ana's heart. Mixed emotions flooded through her as he stood behind her. She felt nothing but empathy for what he was missing, being here devoting his time to others; then a little guilt, and maybe a little envy too at just hearing the child's voice! She'd never heard it, she thought now with a frown, but it resonated somehow. The look on Gabriel's face was one of pure adoration and pride. He was a good father; she'd always known he would be, even if he hadn't exactly planned for that part of his life to start with Ines and an accidental pregnancy. His beautiful heart had propelled him on that journey with Ines anyway.

Why had Ana not made more of an effort to keep in touch with him, to try and meet the person who meant most to him in the whole world? They used to be so close!

'He really is adorable.' She sighed to herself. 'When do you get to hang out with him next?'

'Next weekend, I suppose,' he said. 'He spends half the time with Ines now.'

'And her new husband Pedro,' she added thoughtfully. She could hear in his voice that it bothered him, being away from his son so much.

Gabriel cleared his throat, taking the phone

from her hands. 'What about you?' he asked now.
'Is there anyone special in your life, Miss Independent?'

It was her turn to smirk. 'Me? I don't think so.
Too busy,' she said. As the words left her mouth,
she knew it was a lie. Yes, she was busy, but she
had always *made* herself busy, too determined to
prove she could be something more than what she
assumed people expected her to be, being stuck
in a wheelchair.

Gabriel was cocking his head at her now, looking at her in interest, his brown eyes piercing her
the way they always had. She laughed. 'What?'

'Nothing,' he said quickly, just as a flashback
of them cuddled on the couch hit her from out
of nowhere. She felt herself flushing. The feeling of comfort and safety she had always associated with Gabriel growing up was morphing
into images of things that had never happened.
She'd done that with her last serious boyfriend,
Alberto, not Gabriel—never. She'd have to rein
those thoughts in, if they were going to bump into
each other more now, she thought.

'There was Alberto,' she admitted now. 'In
Bariloche. But he wanted me to move out to the
hills with him and have his babies…'

'Even further out into the hills?' He looked
amused now, and she grimaced.

'I couldn't do it. He was nice but…no. What

would someone like me do in the middle of no-where?' More than that, she found herself think-ing now, Alberto had not been 'the one'. They'd barely had a thing in common besides their lo-cation.

'You'd find something; you always do,' he chided playfully, and she shrugged. Maybe he thought so, but being a parent was tough enough; she couldn't even imagine how someone in a wheelchair would deal with all that without more of a support system around. Gabriel was so lucky having that here. Besides, she *was* busy. All she'd ever wanted was her own clinic. Nothing was going to mess that up now.

Before long, the medical tent was bulging again. At one point they even had a queue outside. All the while, as they worked together and around each other to tend to all manner of minor inju-ries, and finally to release their rehydrated sour grapes back out into the cacophony of music and merriment, Ana couldn't help thinking she had been a bad friend the last five years. She'd gone off and busied herself in all those other places while Gabriel had been going through so much with Javi and Ines.

Working here with Gabriel was great, but the music—the heartbeat of the Carnival—pulsed through the night and only seemed to intensify her guilt. He'd always been there for her and then she'd just disappeared and hooked up with Alberto—probably to take her mind off the whole thing with Gabriel and Ines, now that she really thought about it.

She'd even avoided Gabriel's family on her return visits—out of jealousy, she thought, annoyed with herself. That was the truth of it, really. She hadn't been able to stand seeing him set up home with someone else, let alone with someone he barely knew. Why on earth would she have wanted to watch the whole neighbourhood and all his friends and family coo over them? Yes, she and Gabriel had only ever been friends, but part of her had often thought maybe…*maybe*…something might happen between them, eventually.

'It's getting late; I'm starving,' Gabriel announced when they found themselves alone yet again. Ana was starting to get a bit of a headache from the loud music, but she realised her stomach was growling like a caged monster too. 'I can go get us some snacks, if you don't mind holding the fort.'

'Please,' she said, tidying the last of the gauzes and iodine back into their box. 'Vegan empanada for me,' she added, and he threw her a look.

'Vegan?' He play-gasped. 'Ana, you're breaking my heart!'

She smirked and tutted. He was so dramatic.

'I just don't want to risk eating any meat that's been sitting round all day.'

'That's smart, actually. I'll be straight back.'

Gabriel wasn't even gone three minutes when a shadow appeared in the doorway and two people called her name in unison. She spun round in surprise and felt her eyebrows disappear into her hair as two human bumble bees stepped into the tent, their glittery wings brushing the canvas sides as they shuffled someone else through with them—a little boy dressed as a ladybird.

'It is you, isn't it? Ana! Gabriel said you'd be here tonight. Oh, it's so good to see you! We kind of need your help… Where is Gabriel?'

Ana could hardly believe it. It was Gabriel's mum and dad, sprightly as ever, standing here after all this time. And between them, nursing a grazed knee, was little ladybird Javi.

'I'm so sorry, Gabriel went out for snacks,' she explained, motioning for them to sit the little boy down.

'What's happened here, *mijo?*'

'I fell.'

Quickly she got the gauze back out and told him to sit still as she wiped his wounds gently with antiseptic. All the while, she couldn't help thinking how much he looked like Gabriel: the same mussed black hair fell wildly across his face, like his father's used to when it had been longer, and he'd the same soulful brown eyes. His little brow was furrowed, his eyes screwed up with concentration. He gasped when Ana dabbed the disinfectant onto his skin, then breathed bravely through the sting, blowing bursts of air through his mouth as if he was blowing up an invisible balloon—dramatic, just like Gabriel.

He was looking up at her now, sussing her out, as if realising for the first time that she was different. 'Why are you in a wheelchair?' he asked.

CHAPTER THREE

GABRIEL HAD TAKEN longer than expected getting the snacks, thanks to Carlos Cabrera and his captivating capoeira group. That had taken him completely by surprise—he'd had no idea that the stoic trauma surgeon from the hospital had been so into capoeira, but there he'd been just now, on the side street by the snack stand with his group, drumming up interest for his gym. That had been pretty cool. He could have sworn he'd seen his friend Sofia in the crowd too, too far away for him to call to or reach, but suffice to say it had all been all going on out there and he was later getting back than he'd intended. Was that his parents he could hear…?

Their enthusiasm meant they'd always had the loudest voices of anyone around, but the gap in the blaring music confirmed it was definitely them that he could hear. His heart sped up as he hurried for the doorway of the tent, but when he saw Javi sitting on the chair, talking to Ana, something made him stop and stand back for a second. He couldn't hear what they were saying but Ana seemed to be explaining something about her wheelchair. To his shock, Javi put his arms around Ana, and he watched as she pulled him into a sweet embrace, as if they'd already become firm friends.

'What happened *mijo*?' he demanded, dropping the snacks onto a table and making straight for Javi. His parents stood up from their seats, said his name in unison and he did a double take at their ridiculous outfits.

'I fell, and Ana was just helping me,' his son said, wriggling his knees from his chair, both of which were covered in plasters.

'Nothing too terrible; he'll live,' Ana said, steering her chair back to make more room for him. Gabriel was already on his knees in front of Javi.

'Good thing you knew to come here. We wouldn't want a trail of blood in the parade; it's not Halloween,' he said, making Javi giggle and Ana smirk. He mouthed, 'Thank you!' at her then he pulled his son into a hug, breathing in the familiar scent of his hair, grateful as he always was after a scrape that his son was fine.

He tried never to show it—his son should grow up confident, strong and fearless—but he himself feared something new every day when it came to Javi, especially now the boy lived with Ines and

Pedro most of the time. He thought a lot about that cosy family unit. It was something Gabriel had never been able to give him. Javi wouldn't exactly grow up remembering the short year or so after his birth when he and Ines had bunked up together, trying to make things work for his sake.

'I was on the way to the children's parade when I fell, Papa,' Javi said now, pouting and crossing his arms. The action made a huge dent in the front of his ladybird outfit. 'I'll never get to join the parade now.'

'I'm sorry, *guapo*,' Gabriel sympathised. 'But you had a good time with Grandma and Grandpa, right?'

He nodded a little despondently, and Ana pulled up beside him again. 'Why don't you go?' she suggested to Gabriel, touching his arm. Her slender fingers lingered there for just fraction of a second, but it was long enough for heat to shoot up his forearm and start pumping fresh, hot, new blood to his heart. It was the same as when her eyes had locked on his over Mr Acosta—he hadn't been able to shake how attractive he found her, even more so now that she'd helped Javi.

Gabriel stood up as his mother took to comforting Javier and promising him a story before bed time. 'Go, enjoy what you can of Carnival with him before bed time,' Ana said. 'I'll be fine here, and I should have help soon…'

Just as she said it, Sebastián Lopez, the A&E clinical lead, poked his head round the door, ready for his shift. 'Just in time!' She beamed.

'You have snacks!' Sebastián grinned, high-fiving Gabriel and Javi respectively, before checking out the array of food items on the table.

'Help yourself,' Gabriel offered, still composing himself regarding the strange new heat that had settled around his chest. 'But I'm warning you, there's a vegan item in there.'

Sebastián pulled a face, and Gabriel swung round to Ana. 'Are you sure it's OK if I go?' He studied her deep brown eyes. For some reason, even though he was thrilled to spend at least an hour with Javi before bed time, he was a little reluctant to leave Ana…and it had nothing to do with the fact that he didn't think she could handle things. She could handle anything; it was the thing he admired most about her. It had felt like old times just then, just the two of them dancing on the street, like before she'd left for Bariloche.

'I'm sure. Go.'

Gabriel gathered his things and changed out of his uniform behind the screen, listening to them talking. He remembered more about that night she'd got herself stuck on the beach in Pinamar. That was the night she'd told him she had a job offer in Bariloche.

He'd been crushed. Ines was pregnant and he

was losing his best friend at the time he needed her most. He'd had no idea how to be a father! But then, how could he have asked her to stay? That would have been so selfish. Instead he'd missed her madly, all on his own. Maybe he'd even realised what she'd meant to him, how he'd taken her friendship for granted. He felt so guilty that he'd stopped contacting her once Javi had come along—it wouldn't have been fair to burden her with his problems, not when he'd landed himself in the situation in the first place.

She'd been everywhere before that anyway— or, it seemed like everywhere—while he'd always stayed with his family, where he belonged. It was his place to look out for them and always had been. The Romeros looked out for each other; it was just what they did.

'Go!' Ana laughed now as he hovered around the cabinet, about to put a few more things away.

'OK, OK…bossy as you ever were!' She was practically shooing him out of the door. His parents fussed around her behind him as he took Javi outside. He heard them gushing over how nice it was to have her back after all this time, and how they'd missed seeing her around. Everyone loved Ana. He'd had a pretty hard crush on her once, he mused to himself before shaking it off. No point going there. It wasn't as if he'd ever told his best friend that in the first place. She'd only have rejected him, what with all her plans for global domination.

'Enjoy!' she called to him now, waving at them all, just as he saw Sebastián gag and almost spit something out into his hand.

'He *told* you not to eat the vegan thing,' he heard Ana reprimand him playfully as he, his parents and Javi were swallowed by the crowd again.

The carnival was as crazy as usual as they manoeuvred through a block party, swung past the capoeira demo again and moved out the other end to the kid's carnival. Luckily, Javi seemed to have forgotten the fact that he'd hurt his knees. While they didn't catch the kid's parade, they did forge a path to the funfair for a few games.

'Grandpa, Papa, I want that one!' Javi cried now, jabbing his finger towards a giant stuffed panda hanging above the man behind the mini basketball hoops.

Gabriel and his father exchanged glances. 'Maybe later, Javi,' his father suggested, eyeing his watch. It was almost his bed time, but Gabriel knew that look in his son's eyes. When he wanted something, he wanted it now—a trait he'd inherited from Ines.

The man behind the stand handed Javi a basketball, while pointing towards the hoop at the other side of the booth. Javi missed twice at first, but soon got into a rhythm, and to Gabriel's surprise it wasn't long before he landed three shots in quick succession.

'You're a pro player. Nice one, *mijo*!' He offered a high five, making Javi's ladybird wings knock the hat off a lady nearby, and Javi jumped up and down with excitement as he was handed the large stuffed panda. Javi walked ahead with his grandfather, but Gabriel's mother took his arm, whispering conspiratorially.

'It's so lovely that Ana's back, don't you think?' she said with a sideways smile. 'She was so good with Javi, and she's as pretty as ever. You know, I remember you two running around together before her accident. Such a shame, what happened to her...' She trailed off, shaking her head, and Gabriel frowned.

'It hasn't stopped her doing everything she's always wanted to do,' he found himself saying, as Javi stopped abruptly near the fishing stand and turned to them expectantly. His father promptly handed over the cash for the fishing rod, and Javi went about trying to fish for plastic turtles in an inflatable pond.

'I know, she's always been ambitious,' his mother agreed as they looked at Javi, who was tossing the rod over and over into the water until finally it knocked a small turtle out of the pond completely. 'That new clinic of hers is going to be a lot of work.'

'She has a great team,' Gabriel told her, wondering why he felt obliged to defend her. They were adults now. They weren't on the playground any more, facing the bullies. 'You just watch her, Ma. Dr Az wouldn't have sought her out to take over if she didn't think she could handle it. She always had Ana in mind to run the place after her.'

'I know. Don't you worry; the doctor put in a good word with us too, before she retired. Your father already suggested we keep our medical files with Ana, what with my hernia and his bad knee. It's always been our clinic, but with our family's history maybe now we'll get extra-special attention, huh?'

Gabriel nodded as she spoke about the Romeros' long running friendship with the Mendezes, unable to stop his mind casting back over this evening, working so closely with Ana in the medical tent. He could have sworn he'd felt her eyes on him a lot today, watching him closer than you'd usually watch a work colleague. But things had been pretty hectic, and he hadn't seen her in so long; maybe his mind was playing tricks on him. He might have had a crush on her once, but they'd practically been kids. There was nothing there now, not on her side anyway. She'd been off experiencing the world and was now finally realising her dream of opening her own clinic. The last thing on her mind was hooking up with a child-hood friend and single dad from the same barrio!

His mother was still going on about the time Ana had brought a pot of chicken soup to their door one time she'd been recovering from a cold, when Javi squealed in fresh delight and swung around with a turtle dangling from his fishing line. 'Papa, I caught one!'

'Well done, *mijo*! Now, bed time!' He laughed as Javi skipped ahead with his agile grandfather. Luckily Gabriel's dad was still young enough to keep up with his grandson's enthusiastic endeavours. Javi clutched the panda in his arms tightly, as if it might fly away at any moment, and Gabriel looked on fondly, committing this moment of his young son to memory.

How quickly they grew up. Would Javi even remember the times he spent with him like this, or would he remember his home as being wherever his new family unit was—Ines, Pedro and him? Sometimes he wished he could have made things work with her for his son's sake, but no... Ines and Pedro were perfect for each other. He and Ines had been a completely different story—they were different people.

Somehow, thoughts of Ana kept creeping back in as he took in the colours of the carnival all around them. Maybe it was the colourful way she still dressed... She was a moving rainbow, nothing like the way most other GPs looked, and he admired her for it, breaking the mould under her white coat, and out of it too. Why did healthcare always have to be so dull? She was who she was, at work and at home. Did she consider this her home, now that she was back? Would she stay? Did she want a family some day?

Why are you even thinking all this, Gabriel?

He couldn't get her out of his head now—her colourful presence, her reassuring smile and her easy manner with Javi. Today it had hit home just how much he'd missed being around her all this time. And she really had seemed to hit it off with Javi.

As he tucked Javi up in bed, the little boy asked him about Ana.

'She said she had a car accident and that's why she's on wheels,' he said, frowning.

'It's a wheelchair, Javi,' Gabriel corrected him, listening to his parents shuffling around downstairs, still wearing their bumble bee outfits and making each other laugh.

'She said I must always wear a seatbelt.'

'And she's right,' he said with a sigh, getting back to the book he was reading. How could he help the fact that his mind was only half on the book now? He was thinking about the accident, the car wreck that had torn Ana's life to shreds

when she'd been a kid and had damaged her spinal cord beyond repair. His parents had taken
him to visit her in hospital, and he hadn't been
able to comprehend it at the time, the fact that
his best friend might not be able to walk again.
She'd always been a faster runner than him: racing ahead on the track during sports class; sprinting for the school bus at his side before hopping
on first every time, always in a hurry to get somewhere—always in a hurry to get *everywhere*,
with or without him.

Two months after the accident, when she'd
finally come home from hospital for good, his
whole family had gone to her house to welcome
her back. The first time they'd seen her pale
face and frail frame, being lifted from the ambulance and lowered into the wheelchair outside
her house, his mother had started sniffing behind
her bouquet of peonies, and it had only really hit
him then exactly what had happened to Ana. He'd
felt it like a switch. The gravity had been sucked
out from all around him and, when he'd met her
eyes, he'd seen only a shadow of his friend.

The younger him had never showed how
shocked, sad and sorry for her he really was,
though. He'd known enough then to know that
wasn't what she needed. Instead, from that very
day, when he'd taken the flowers from his mother's hands and marched ahead of them all up to

the front door, he'd made it his job to make her life easier in any way he could.

Only, Ana had never really needed him to do that for her. She'd made it a point not to need *anyone* over the years, to do everything herself that any able-bodied person could do and more. She'd never stopped running, really. There was always some place she had to be, with him or without him—mostly without him. And he'd always let her go. More than that, he'd encouraged her!

In later years, he'd sometimes wondered if his one-man best-friend support system had been an act, a cover up, some kind of disguise he'd just kept putting on every day so she wouldn't see the real him. The real him, who had sometimes looked at her as more than a friend—as *his*, somehow—but she would never have felt the same way about him.

Turning out the light on a sleepy Javi's nightstand, he had a sudden flashback of doing the same thing to Ana's light the night he'd taken her home blind drunk after she'd graduated medical school. She still didn't know how long he'd stayed there, watching over her while she'd slept, wishing he could just curl up beside her and go to sleep instead of being the gentleman and making his way home.

Sometimes he'd been so confused about his feelings for Ana, and so certain she'd reject him if he tried anything at all, that he'd hooked up with other people right in front of her just to cover the tracks of his crush.

Maybe that was why he'd slept with Ines in the first place, he considered now. It was hard to remember, exactly—it had all been such a whirlwind—but, thinking back, the look on Ana's face in the car the whole way to the Pinamar that day had not been one of excitement...and hadn't that been the first time she'd met Ines? He could remember being acutely aware of Ana there, watching them. Could remember the way his heart had sped up at the notion that she might be...jealous. What could he have done by that point, though? Ines had already been pregnant and his hands were tied.

And on that same trip, Ana had announced she was leaving for Bariloche. It was funny—and kind of troubling at the same time—that even now, even after spending the last five years apart, Ana was having the same effect on his heart.

The sound of slow, romantic love songs crept up the stairs as he left Javi's room. Deciding that his parents were probably doing something cute, such as dancing together in their bumble bee costumes, he called goodnight to them, went into his own room and lay down on the bed, picking up his book. They would let themselves out the way they always did—his family were used to coming and going as they pleased.

But Gabriel didn't even get to finish one chapter before he was fast asleep and dreaming of being back in Ana's bedroom. This time, however, he was very much in the bed with her. He was not just keeping an eye on his sleeping friend from the doorway. And Ana was very much awake and doing wicked things to him in return.

CHAPTER FOUR

GABRIEL WAS JOLTED awake by his phone trilling from the nightstand. He blinked, eyes adjusting to the darkness, and glanced at the clock: four-forty-five. 'So early,' he mumbled to himself, groping for the phone with one hand and swinging his legs over the side of the bed. His dreams about Ana played on in his head as he said a sleepy hello. Blinking again, his heart jolted into his throat as an unmistakeable Ana replied.

'Gabriel?' She sounded frantic and spoke so fast he could barely keep up. 'I'm sorry, I know it's so early—I wouldn't have called, except it's an emergency. My healthcare assistant was knocked out by an octopus…'

'An octopus?' he blurted, trying not to laugh despite the hour *and* the unwelcome thoughts about this very woman that he still couldn't shake, especially as she spoke to him while he was still in bed.

'Someone dressed as an octopus, last night at Carnival,' she explained. 'Swept her off her feet in all the wrong ways—she's dislocated her arm. We don't know how long she'll be out of action.'

He raked a hand through his dishevelled hair, catching sight of himself in the long mirror by the wardrobe. 'And you need me to cover?'

'We open tomorrow, Gabriel, and my appointment book is full. I can't go cancelling on people in my first week, but I need a locum. It'll take some time to find one, but in the meantime, didn't you say something about having some time off while Bruno trains the new recruits?'

Gabriel paused and crossed to the window. He probably had; they'd spoken about all kinds of things in the medical tent between tending to all those minor casualties. Except what he'd wanted to say, of course: the fact that she was still one of the most bewitching people he'd ever had the fortune to stand beside. Oh, Lord, those dreams had got to him more than he'd thought!

'That's right.'

'You know I wouldn't ask unless I needed you.'

He bit back a smile, studying the street outside. It was empty, except for one solo dog-walker illuminated under a streetlamp. He didn't know whether to be happy she'd thought of him first, or annoyed, because now, of course, he couldn't say no. With no ambulance shifts for the week, he'd thought maybe he would take his camper van out to Playa Varese, one of the most well-known beaches along the Mar del Plata waterfront, and maybe do a little fishing. Or see if he couldn't wrangle some more time with Javi, if Ines would allow it outside of his allocated weekends... But now Ana needed him.

'Gabe?'

'OK!' A surge of adrenaline rocketed through him, waking him up properly as his brain attempted to process the enormity of the request, on top of the fact that he'd said OK on autopilot. What the...? 'Yes,' he said groggily. 'Yes, of course I'll help you, Ana.'

Ana breathed a sigh of relief that he felt though to his core, and immediately he knew he'd made the right choice. Ana had never found it easy asking for help. She always had to do everything by herself or she labelled herself a failure, somehow, she'd told him one night before he'd met Ines.

'Thank you so much,' she said. 'I knew I could count on you. I'll make it up to you, I promise.'

There was a pause. Gabriel shuffled barefoot as the details of his dream came flooding back. She'd already made it up to him in his subconscious and she didn't even know—should he feel *guilty* for the fact that his dream self had just had sex with his friend?

'I'll text you the details later this morning,' she said finally. 'We'll make it work.'

'Get some sleep,' he told her, realising suddenly

that she must not have slept all night, panicking before deciding to call him.

'You know me—I don't sleep when I've got something on my mind.' Gabriel nodded, smiling to himself. He still knew her so well, even after all this time.

When they'd hung up, he reckoned it was pointless trying to go back to sleep. Besides, he couldn't get the very intricate, highly intimate details of his dreams to leave his mind. They played on persistently as he flipped on the coffee pot, and swiped up the newspaper just as it was shoved through his letterbox. So much for his time off, he thought, dropping to the seat at the dining table and staring unseeingly at the paper. Still, at least Javi would be taken care of while he acted as locum for Ana at the new clinic. He was meant to be with Ines all week anyway—and Pedro, he thought begrudgingly, sloshing coffee into his well-loved *Happy Birthday* mug.

Ines and Pedro would have all kinds of adventures lined up for him already. She rarely told him what they were, exactly, until after the fact, although she frequently demanded to know exactly what *he* had planned for Javi's visits with *him*. She'd always struggled to leave Javi with his parents and him, even though she knew he was perfectly safe and content with them. She was the doting mother he'd always known she would be, ever since she'd looked at that positive pregnancy test and had told him flat out she was keeping the baby.

Every time he thought of the day she might demand full custody of their son was enough to make him shudder. Ever since she'd blown up that time when she'd bumped into Javi with his grandparents in the toy shop, he'd been petrified of putting a foot wrong. Oh, she had not been impressed that day! But it hadn't been his fault—it wasn't as if he'd asked for that family's car to crash outside the church gates…

Gabriel had been supposed to look after Javi that afternoon, and they'd been having a great time, but car crashes were the worst—not least because they always reminded him of what had happened to Ana. What was he supposed to have done except ask his parents to step in while he raced to the scene to join Bruno? His parents never minded stepping in at short notice. They lived for spending time with their grandson. But Ines hadn't seemed to understand that. She said the boy needed stability…which was true.

Every time he thought of his sweet little son in that tight, happy, stable family unit of three, in flooded the river of remorse at not being able to offer him the same thing. Ines deserved happiness—she was a great woman and an excellent mother—but all he wanted was to be a great father too. And, right now, he couldn't help fearing that Javi might grow up *wanting* to be with Ines and Pedro full-time.

At least his mind would be taken off that worry all this week working with Ana, he thought, swigging his coffee before realising with a sigh that he might have a whole new set of worries to contend with, now that Ana was back in his life. If those dreams were anything to go by, she'd stirred something up in his subconscious that was very much pleasure-related, not business.

Gabriel couldn't read one paragraph of the newspaper now. Now that he'd entertained the notion that he found Ana attractive, it was almost impossible to stop his mind wandering. But wondering if that connection would ever make it from his dreams into reality was pointless— Ana was far too much of a free spirit ever to be with someone so tied down! He would just have to keep his dream self in check, and make sure she never got wind of this unfortunate attraction.

The clinic was buzzing with energy on the first Monday of opening, and the staff was rushed off its feet on the new, squeaky-clean floors. It was only mid-morning, but to Ana it felt as if they'd been going for hours already. Still, without Gabriel she would have been way more stressed by now, she thought, casting her eye to where he was on the phone. He'd taken a short break to answer a call. He seemed quite pleased about something, from what she could hear, and his smile was contagious.

'What's going on?' she asked, intrigued.

'Sofia and Carlos, two friends from the hospital, that's what.' He grinned and she cocked her head, confused. 'Trauma loves trauma, what more can I say?' he added with a mischievous smirk. 'Rumour has it they got together at the carnival, but she's not letting on to *me*. That's so Fia! I'm having to hear it from Bruno. He says good luck, by the way.'

'Good luck?' Ana was distracted now.

He looked so cute when he was energised and excited, like the teenage Gabe who'd pushed her chair through the crowds of Defensa Street that time she'd been hell-bent on buying the perfect painting from one of her favourite street artists.

Ana was about to ask more about this rumoured new couple when an elderly man swung through the door and almost stumbled. Gabriel was there in a flash and, as she sprang into action beside him, she tried her best not to think about the way she'd felt in that medical tent, meeting Javi. She'd been almost jealous! It had stunned her, being jealous of Gabriel being a parent, of having something so wonderful, stable and joyous in his life as a much-loved child. He deserved it, but she realised she'd missed a lot while she'd been away.

Still, thank goodness he'd agreed to help out at the clinic. They would have more chances to catch up, maybe rebuild some of the friendship that had broken down. Her assistant Carla would be out for a while with her injuries, but he'd been so cool about covering. His calm, kind and compassionate assistance was a godsend in this frenetic environment, and he'd already helped quite a few patients feel more relaxed both before and during their appointments. She'd almost forgotten, until today, that he had a special ability to explain medical concepts in layman's terms. It made even the most nervous patient feel as if they could trust him implicitly.

Just then, something caught her eye. Ana noticed a woman in her mid-twenties looking uncharacteristically anxious, biting on her nails and fidgeting in her seat. The young brunette was alone, and Ana knew she was waiting for her appointment. She quickly made her way over to her, noting she was looking so anxious, she probably wanted nothing more than to run away.

'Are you all right?' Ana asked gently. The woman, a local called Catalina, looked up at her with an almost desperate expression.

'I thought I could do this,' Catalina told her, her voice coming out choked. 'I thought it would be easy for me to get through the check-up, but now I'm here, I think I'm too scared.'

'That's totally understandable,' said Gabriel, appearing behind her with a smile, a clipboard tucked under his arm. 'It can be hard when you don't know what to expect.'

Ana released a breath. His deep voice had a soothing quality that not only calmed *her* on the spot, it instantly seemed to put Catalina at ease too.

Ana's receptionist, Maria, called her to tend to another patient, but she couldn't help glancing over in admiration as Gabriel began talking to Catalina in earnest about her worries, asking what he could do to help alleviate all her concerns about having her first set of tests done at the clinic. She was here to see if they could determine what was causing her excruciating stomach pains, and she'd already self-diagnosed herself on the Internet, which had only ended up exacerbating her anxiety.

He was listening attentively without judgement or criticism, nodding encouragingly when Catalina shared what Ana knew must have been uncomfortable thoughts or feelings about being there. Eventually, she wheeled back over, just in time to hear him conclude their conversation with one final, friendly remark. 'Remember—we are here for you, all of us, no matter what happens.'

'I'm so glad I was referred to this clinic,' Catalina told him warmly in response. 'I can tell you have an amazing team.'

Ana felt her heart swell and her cheeks flushed when Gabriel caught her watching him. It was just that he was so handsome, and even more so now that his gentle manner seemed to have erased any doubt from this patient's panicked mind. Even later in the private consultation room, when Ana informed her that it looked like endometriosis and further tests from a specialist would confirm it, Catalina seemed calm and in control, and accepting of the fact that she was in good hands, no matter what.

The afternoon went by quickly, and Ana found herself looking forward to the times she and Gabriel were alone with the patients. He was proving himself to be just as helpful as she'd initially suspected he would be, but she was a little annoyed at how her heart seemed to beat just that little bit faster every time he walked by or threw a smile her way. *Cut out this crush—nothing can come of it,* she reminded herself sternly for what felt like the hundredth time that very hour. Gabriel was out of her league. He went for artistic, designer-clothes-clad women like Ines…or at least, he used to, she thought now. Something hadn't worked out between them or they'd still be together, raising Javi.

Javi was *everything* to him, she thought as she welcomed a male patient in his sixties into the consultation room. Gabriel was already there, studying the man's medical chart, just transferred over from his last clinic.

Gabriel had a lot going on, juggling his career with being Javi's doting dad, and he didn't need a romance complicating his life, especially not with her. He needed a friend, not some busy woman with a demanding new position in the community, with barely enough time to do her laundry, let alone arrange a date. They had always been just friends anyway, she thought sadly, remembering Ines's hands in his hair on that car ride to the beach. Ana was his friend—that was all he'd ever seen her as.

Ana steered her chair behind the desk. Gabriel helped her adjust it quietly, then stepped back quickly, as if he'd intruded. 'It's OK,' she mouthed at him, touched as their patient looked between them for a moment with a wry smile on his thin lips. What were these feelings?

Suddenly the man bent over in obvious pain, and Gabriel hurried to help him into a chair.

'Mr Hernandez,' she began gently, once he was settled in the char, still wincing almost apologetically, 'I can see you're in a lot of discomfort; does your back hurt?'

'A lot…' The poor man breathed, producing a

polka-dotted handkerchief from his pocket and mopping his brow with it.

'We're here to help you, and we'll do our best to find out what's going on,' she said.

Mr Hernandez nodded, his face etched with pain. 'It's my age, doctor, that's what's going on,' he mumbled, and she ordered him to lie down so Gabriel could examine him. She watched his warm, brown eyes crinkle at the edges. Javi had exactly the same eyes.

'Let's work out what's causing this pain, shall we, sir?' he said now, and Ana couldn't help but steal more than a few glances at him as he ran the stethoscope over the older man's chest and felt about his lower abdomen for any swellings. Whenever their eyes briefly locked, the flutter in her chest took her by surprise again, a sensation she did her best to try and ignore, but totally failed to. This was already getting uncomfortable. Where was the off button for this attraction?

'Based on your symptoms,' he continued minutes later, 'It seems likely that your pain is musculoskeletal, particularly related to your lower back muscles. Doctor, what do you think?'

Ana nodded. 'Small, specific exercises will help, and we can certainly have our expert put a programme together.'

Ana wheeled to the store cabinet she had ensured was at just the right height to enable her to reach everything alone from her wheelchair. 'We'll start you on a physical therapy regimen, Mr Hernandez,' she said as Gabriel offered his assistance to her. She brushed him off, gathering some pain medication, letting him know she didn't need his help. 'Our nurse will provide you with exercises to do at home. In the meantime, we'll give you something to alleviate your pain, how about that?'

When she turned, Gabriel was standing back again, as if he was wholly embarrassed to have tried to help her. She apologised by way of a look and he sighed, frowning to himself. Shoot, had she just been too defensive? He *knew* she hated people feeling that they had to help her, but the tension between them was palpable now. What was happening? This was in no way an emergency case, the likes of which he dealt with every day on paramedic duty, but her heart continued to thrash at her ribs like a wind-ravaged branch as she explained the kind of low-key physical exercises the nurse was likely to suggest, and she could've sworn Gabriel could hear it.

He saw Mr Hernandez out while she swept the sheet from the bed, ready to replace it for the next patient. She mumbled softly to herself the whole time, 'What is wrong with you, Ana?' This was so confusing. Moments later, Gabriel was back in the room, closing the door behind him softly.

Her chest heaved with the sudden wild dance of her heart.

'I'm sorry, Ana,' he said quietly, fixing his eyes on hers. 'I remember how annoyed you always used to get when people tried to help you. I shouldn't…'

'It's OK.'

'It's really not,' he said, stepping closer so that only the empty bed was between them. Her heart was trying to escape through her throat. 'You had this whole place specially designed so you could manage it yourself.'

'I never intended to handle *everything* alone, Gabriel,' she snapped back.

He narrowed his soulful eyes and dashed a hand along his jaw just as the door opened behind them. The severity of her own words and tone shocked her as she cleared her throat self-consciously.

Maria stuck her head in. 'Should I send your next patient in, Ana?' she said, looking between them with interest.

Ana caught the flicker of a knowing smile on her receptionist's face as Gabriel walked past her, saying he'd get the patient from the waiting room.

'What's going on with you two?' Maria asked when Gabriel was gone.

'Who, Gabriel? Nothing.' Ana's pulse quickened as she said it, turning her back to Maria in the chair so she couldn't see her reddening cheeks.

'You make a good team. Does that sizzling chemistry extend beyond these walls?'

Sizzling chemistry? Ana rolled her eyes.

'We're just friends,' she said loudly, just to make her point crystal clear to herself, as well as Maria. This had to stop; it was already getting ridiculous!

The next thing she knew, Maria had closed the door behind her, and Ana was left wondering how on earth she'd get through the week like this.

CHAPTER FIVE

THINGS HAD CHANGED so quickly in the city after Carnival, Gabriel thought, locking his front door behind him. The streets that had been bustling with life and snap-happy tourists were now empty at this early hour, apart from the occasional late-night reveller who hadn't made it home before sunrise. Rising above the stillness of the streets, the sound of blaring sirens hit his ears as he walked past the cemetery. It made him picture Bruno out there, training his new intake of paramedics. He'd been talking to Sofia about the drama at the hospital over Carnival, and about her blossoming love for Carlos—good for her! While he'd missed the action sometimes, the slower pace of the clinic and its significant lack of emergency patients and trauma was kind of refreshing.

He was just thinking how quickly this week had gone, in the presence of Ana and all these new clients of hers, when a noise from up ahead caught his ears. The clinic wasn't even open yet, but someone was outside, and a frantic cry cut through the peaceful morning air.

'Help! Somebody, please help!' a young woman's voice cried out, her desperation piercing his heart as he sprinted faster towards the locked clinic. Ana got there at the exact same time, the coffee she'd been balancing between her knees wobbling precariously as she stopped her chair short in front of the woman. Gabriel exchanged a quick glance with her before the young woman with dishevelled chestnut hair started gasping wildly for breath.

'Anaphylactic shock,' he said in sync with Ana, whose eyes widened before narrowing sharply. Her coffee fell to the floor, splattering the pavement with brown liquid.

'Help!' The girl clutched at her throat, her face twisted in panic as she struggled to breathe. Her skin had paled to an eerie shade of blue in the last two seconds, and her eyes pleaded for salvation. Gabriel caught her just as she was about to hit the pavement. He and Ana were right—he'd seen this reaction before.

Ana fumbled for her keys and her phone at the same time while he held the woman on his lap on the ground. 'I'm a paramedic. My name's Gabriel. What's your name?'

The girl's voice, weak and trembling, managed to stammer out, 'M-Melissa...'

Ana was already on her phone, dialling for an ambulance. Maria arrived now, early for her shift. She raced ahead into the clinic to fetch blankets as Ana held the phone to her ear. 'We need an ambulance at City Clinic, a possible anaphylactic shock. Send it right away!'

'Please, help me,' Melissa begged, her voice rasping as her breathing grew more laboured.

'Melissa, we're going to help you,' Ana said quickly as Gabriel patted her down and checked her purse quickly for an epi-pen. 'We think you're having a severe allergic reaction. Try to stay calm. Do you have anything on you for these reactions?'

'I don't see anything,' Gabriel answered for her. With a nod to Ana to stay with her and keep her calm, he rushed inside for an epinephrine auto-injector. On his return, Ana held Melissa steady while he got to his knees and carefully administered the life-saving medication into her thigh. The tension was palpable as they waited for the epinephrine to take effect and Ana's eyes were hard and focused even as a small crowd gathered round on the street, looking on at them.

Seconds stretched into agonising minutes, but finally Melissa's breathing started to ease. The bluish tint to her skin began to recede, and her desperate gasps turned into shuddering sobs of relief, just as the ambulance screeched round the corner. Bruno and one of his new recruits jumped out.

Ana was still laser-focused on the girl. 'Better?' she asked, her voice gentle and reassuring as Gabriel joined her.

Melissa nodded, tears streaming down her face. 'Thank you, thank you so much. It came on so fast... I couldn't find my phone, I just stumbled straight here, I wasn't thinking...'

Gabriel updated Bruno and his co-dispatcher on Melissa's condition. 'The epinephrine seems to be helping. But you should take her anyway, give her a proper check-up. Poor girl's in shock.'

Melissa's grip on Ana's hand remained tight as she struggled to regain her composure. 'I... I've never had a reaction like this before. I don't even know what triggered it.'

'They'll find out at the hospital,' Ana said, and Gabriel nodded, helping the girl to her feet with Bruno.

Ana offered a comforting smile from her wheelchair. 'Sometimes, allergies can develop suddenly. The most important thing is that you got help in time.'

'Thanks to you two,' she said, her voice laden with relief as she looked between them in gratitude.

Melissa, now in even more capable hands, was quickly loaded into the ambulance, where Bruno's assistant fitted an oxygen mask. Bruno took Gabriel aside. 'Good thing you were there, and Ana too. Who'd have thought the clinic would have you on your toes as much as being out with me?'

Gabriel smirked, glancing back at Ana, who was shooing away the crowds as politely as she could. 'I know, right?'

'So, how long before you ask her out?' Bruno asked quietly.

'What?' Gabriel frowned.

'Oh, come on, we all know that's why you agreed to help her out—you like her! I always knew you two had a connection. Are you...you know...exploring it now, finally?'

Gabriel shook his head at his old friend, hoping Ana hadn't heard. 'We're just friends, Bruno.'

Bruno slapped his shoulder playfully before hopping back into the ambulance. Gabriel watched as the vehicle sped away, pondering his colleague's words. *Exploring* it? As if: Ana only saw him as a friend!

'I hope she'll be okay,' Ana murmured behind him.

Gabriel put a reassuring hand on her shoulder, then removed it quickly. 'We did everything we could. She'll get the care she needs now. As for you, I think you need a new coffee!'

He went for their coffees in the adrenaline-charged aftermath, his mind racing, remembering the look on Bruno's face just now, and the tone of Ana's voice that first day: *we're just friends.*

She'd spoken so loudly to Maria that the whole waiting room could have heard, if they'd been interested. Thankfully they hadn't been; he was quite sure of that. No one had ever been as interested in Ana and him as *he* had, not that anything had ever happened. She'd always been so invested in her career and maintaining her fierce independence, and she was no different now. He'd always been the guy who'd never leave the city, who'd never crave adventure the way she did, who was happy to stay close in the loving embrace of his happy family circle.

Then he'd grown the biggest roots of all, stronger roots than his family had ever given him: he'd become a dad.

Stopping for their coffees at his usual street vendor, he couldn't help thinking about how Javi had reacted to Ana the first time he'd met her. He had asked about her since, on last night's video call: 'Where's that nice lady in the wheelchair?'

Funny, he had never really focused on Ana's chair at all, maybe because he'd known her before her accident, but even afterwards, when she'd become the bubbly, popular kid in the barrio, always dancing round the tables with him at the endless *asados.*

Back at the clinic, Gabriel watched her for a moment through the glass doors, noting the way her red flowery headband caught the sun, like her matching flats, as she busied herself with rearranging the leaves on a fern on a shelf and adjusting a chair in alignment with the rest. She looked anxious now. Maybe she was waiting for the next patient, or thinking about something else.

Spotting him, she waved and he stepped inside. 'Hi,' he said, handing over one of the *café con leches*.

'You're so thoughtful,' she said with a broad smile, though he could tell she was still a little anxious about something—most likely Melissa, he thought. He pulled out a bag of sweet *alfajors* next— a crumbly cookie made with flour, oozing *dulce de leche*—and watched her eyes widen as he gave her one in a napkin.

'This is new,' she said, eyebrows raised at the offering.

'Well, it's Friday,' he reasoned.

She cocked her head and studied him a moment as he stood in front of her, and he felt her weighing something up. 'I can't thank you enough for helping me out this week. I know you probably had other things to do, places to be.'

He shrugged, walking past her to drop his bag behind Reception. He'd used some of his holiday allowance to be here, not that he'd told her that.

She might not have allowed him to come otherwise. 'You know Bruno didn't need me this week; he has that whole new intake of paramedics to order around. I thought it might be nice for *you* to order me around instead.'

'It was. It is,' she said, and she laughed nervously. 'Can you spare some more time for me?' she asked.

Aha! So that was it....

'My assistant is still out injured, and we don't know when she'll be able to return. I'm looking for another locum but...'

'I can stay a little longer,' he said, probably too quickly, now that he thought about it. What was a few more leave days anyway? He had loads of them to use up, and he'd still have plenty left to spend with Javi another time. It wasn't as though he ever went very far.

'You're a life saver. Literally.'

'I know you'll make it up to me.' He watched her smile, just as he smirked, remembering his dream. She was still making it up to him at times in their nightly rendezvous! What would she say if he told her?

For a second he wanted to tell her, to see if she'd laugh and call him an idiot, or remind him tartly that he was her friend, and now colleague, and that he shouldn't go there. Instead he just watched her rosy-red lips as she took a small, bird-like bite of the *alfajor*. In his dreams he had nibbled her bottom lip and woken up still tasting it…wanting it for real. Wanting her, all of her.

Suddenly having the reception desk between them felt safer. Ana seemed to sense the tension that he felt rising and she put down her *alfajor*, patting at her lips self-consciously.

'So, how's Javi doing?' she asked, glancing at the clock. Trust it to be a quiet morning, now that the action of their earlier shock patient was over. He squared his shoulders, still fighting off the desire to lick the taste of *alfajor* from her bottom lip.

'He's great. He's been with Ines and his stepdad all week, and he will be most of next week too.' As he said it, the familiar twinge of annoyance took hold. Their home had become Javi's base instead of his. He had him tomorrow, though, which he told Ana.

'Does Javi call Ines's partner his stepdad?' Ana asked curiously.

Gabriel studied her a moment. That red headband really suited her. 'I don't think Javi refers to him as that, no,' he admitted. 'But that's what Pedro is—they're married, after all. And Javi spends a lot of time with them.'

'More than with you?'

He shuffled on his feet. 'Some weeks, yes. Pedro works from home as a software engineer, so he can be a lot more flexible with his schedule than me. He's building Javi a treehouse in the yard.'

Ana chewed her lip, staring at him. Gabriel realised a little bitterness might have escaped with his words. He probably wouldn't know the first thing about building a treehouse. He used his hands to help sick people, which he'd take over having carpentry skills any day, but it didn't exactly do much to excite a little boy.

Thankfully the door opened behind him then. In walked their first official patient of the day, a girl who looked about ten years old, accompanied by her worried-looking mother. They learned her name was Lily, and her eyes and nose held the tell-tale redness indicative of a cold.

'Hello, Lily,' Gabriel said, offering a warm smile as Ana welcomed them straight into the consultation room, discreetly placing her *alfajor* behind the reception desk on the way past.

In the room, Lily sniffed and looked up at them both, while her mother took the comfy leather chair by the window. Her head was haloed immediately by a vase of fresh marigolds.

'She says her throat hurts, and she can't stop coughing,' the woman explained. At that, the young girl started hacking wildly, banging on her chest.

'It's like there's something stuck in there,' she gasped between coughs.

Ana, with her usual comforting presence, pulled up beside Lily and pressed the stethoscope to her chest. Gabriel itched to swipe an illicit crumb that had landed quietly on the lapel of her white coat. 'We're here to help you, sweetie. How long has this been bothering you?'

Lily started to speak, but her voice was raspy and her mother cut in again. 'I had a fever last week, then her brother got sick; it's been going around their school.'

Ana threw him a look over the girl's head. He could tell she was thinking, if that was the case, they might soon have quite a few sick children coming in. Already his mind was churning. If Javi caught it, would he even be able to see him at the weekend, or would Ines keep him with her, as she'd tried to the last time he'd got sick? Javi had asked for his papa, but apparently Ines had told the little boy that he had to stay put with Pedro and her until he was better. Gabriel had felt so guilty for not being able to offer him the same amount of creature comforts, that he'd shown up unannounced with a toy robot. Ines had let him in, of course, albeit reluctantly.

'My chest feels so tight,' Lily managed. Gabriel could relate. If Javi was ever sick again he'd want to be there, but would he even be told about it? Ines wasn't cruel but she just wouldn't think to involve him. She would probably assume he was too busy, that she and Pedro could manage, and that was what bothered him the most.

Ana was still holding the stethoscope to Lily's chest, assessing her shallow breaths. 'Well, I can tell there's some congestion in your lungs,' she said, her soft hand resting on Lily's shoulder. 'Gabriel here will do a throat swab, and we'll run some tests to confirm, but it seems like you have a respiratory infection. It's nothing to worry about.'

As Lily coughed and winced, Ana exchanged another glance with Gabriel before he turned to prepare the swab, accidentally knocking a file to the floor. Swiping it up, he could feel her eyes on him, even as she talked with Lily's mother. Did she know something was bothering him? Maybe he'd opened up too much before about Ines and Pedro. It wasn't her problem—she had enough going on her own life.

But, despite that, this chemistry between them was building by the second, even with patients in the same room. They'd been doing a silent dance of shared glances and unspoken words all week and he wasn't quite sure how to feel about it. It wasn't exactly professional…but, despite that, he liked working with her. They made a good team. And, now that he'd willingly extended his time as her assistant, he would have to try even harder to keep this attraction hidden, he thought to him-self, crinkling up his nose.

Way to go, Gabe!

Together, they completed the examination, he doing the swab, she taking notes and discussing possible medications Lily could collect without a prescription from the pharmacy. They saw Lily and her mother out at the front door and Ana turned to him.

'We make a good team, don't we, you and I?' he got out quickly, because he'd just been think-ing it. She smiled in the sunlight and adjusted her headband self-consciously.

'I was thinking the same thing,' she replied. He could have sworn he saw a flush starting to spread across her cheeks before she hid it behind her hair. The same kind of look he'd probably had on his face, talking to her on the phone just after that dream about her. Had she also been feeling that this was somehow…different this time? No. He was reading too much into it.

Ana put a hand on his arm. 'You looked a bit… I don't know…distant in there, when she said there was something going around the school. Were you worried about Javi?'

He stared at her, thrown. *How did she know?* Her large brown eyes sparkled with a warmth he suddenly wanted to keep on sinking into. 'I… I don't even know if they go to the same school, but yes, I was thinking about him,' he admitted with a sigh. 'If he gets sick, I'm not able to be there for him the way Ines and Pedro are.'

'That's not your fault, is it? You work hard doing irregular hours, it's the nature of your job. And they're a *couple*, whereas you're…'

'I'm just a single dad,' he finished for her.

Ana screwed up her nose. 'That's not what I meant… I mean, it's not a bad thing being a single dad, is it?'

Maria's eyes were on them again from behind the desk. If only he could stroll to the door and gulp in some fresh air. She'd touched a sore point, not that she knew it. Well, she hadn't till now.

Ana's fingers were still pressed to his arm, holding him in place. 'Javi knows you're a great papa,' she told him, eyeing him in a way that made him ache to sweep back from her face the stray strand of hair that had escaped from her headband. 'I've met him, remember.'

Of course he remembered. Javi still talked about her. But Gabriel just nodded, feeling more than a little uncomfortable all of a sudden, and not just because Maria was watching this all play out whilst tapping at the keyboard with audible efficiency. The last thing he wanted was for Ana to feel bad for him in any way or, heaven forbid, sorry for him. He was doing fine for the most part, and he was here to help *her*, not the other way around!

Besides, she'd made it clear to Maria what she thought of him—they were just friends. He would do well to remember that, he told himself, even if she appeared to see him, really *see* him, for once. This was something new and intriguing, and which he'd never really experienced with anyone else. Most women he'd tried to date after Ines had either been uninterested in Javi, or indifferent to Gabriel's chosen career—or both—so any chemistry he might have felt had always fizzled out after a few encounters.

Was that chemistry he could feel now, sending heatwaves up his arm at Ana's touch? He withdrew his arm quickly and raked his hair back, avoiding her questioning gaze. Maybe it was, maybe it wasn't, but this was getting out of hand. How much longer could he keep this up, resisting the urge to make a move? Welcome relief flooded through him again when their next appointment walked through the door.

A bad case of heartburn, a sprained wrist and a plastic brick getting stuck somewhere it shouldn't have been consumed the rest of the day and afternoon. Ana couldn't help feel a slight pang of excitement that Gabriel had agreed to work at the clinic for a few more days; they really did work so well together, and there wasn't a patient who entered the building who didn't like him. He was charming, kind and affable to the point of adorable, but there was something else about him that drew her in, and kept on drawing her in, the more she was around him—a kind of sadness that seeped through that cheerful exterior and shone in his warm brown eyes when he talked about Javi.

Maybe he felt a little helpless that he couldn't give Javi what Ines could, she thought, watching him now with a ten-year-old boy who was waiting for his mother, reading a comic.

Maybe he genuinely thought it wasn't an attractive quality, being a single dad, which was ridiculous! Not only was he the most handsome man around for miles, he was also a great father. How could he think he wasn't, just because he wasn't married, as Ines was? A thought struck her. Maybe he didn't *want* to be single. Frowning to herself, she realised the thought of him with anyone made her feel quite nauseous. Thinking about it, she'd been too chicken to ask about his love life after Ines in case he admitted he'd had feelings for someone else.

Stupid! They were friends and that was that. He'd seemed a little down about that treehouse, though, she pondered as the child's face lit up. Gabriel had handed him another comic and told

him he could keep it. She wondered what Pedro
was like. Maybe he'd taken on the stepdad role
with such gusto that Gabriel truly thought he
couldn't keep up.

Still, it wasn't a matter for her to get involved
in, she thought suddenly, catching herself getting
flustered on his behalf; there was enough going
on in her own life. She didn't have the time to
get involved in his, even if she was now wondering what she could do to make him feel special,
in case he didn't realise it himself. She'd made
him feel pretty special in her dream last night...
But then, her dream self was often a wanton sex
goddess—probably because she hadn't seen any
action in a long time! If it hadn't been Gabriel
in her dream, it would have been someone else,
she reminded herself. It was only him because
he was on her mind, and at her side all the time
after having been apart for so long.

She hadn't had dreams like that in a long time,
though. No one else had ruffled her this much
and got her mind churning. Her subconscious was
really doing a number on her!

When the last patient was out of the door, Ana
made a point to lock it quickly and turn back to
her team.

'Well, that was a successful first week, everyone! I think we deserve a night out to celebrate.
What do you say?'

She looked expectantly between Maria and Gabriel, hoping they'd see her enthusiasm and agree. Obviously they were all tired, herself included, but she wanted to treat them all, now more than ever. Secretly she wasn't ready for the day to be over, or to go home alone to her apartment and another box of her mum's leftovers. When was the last time she'd eaten anywhere but her apartment? Hard to remember; there was always some new file or document to read at the dinner table. Most of the time she barely remembered eating, as she did it so often on autopilot.

Gabriel looked a little reluctant. A shiver of disappointment travelled through her bones, though she didn't let it show on her face. Thankfully, Maria was waving her phone in the air enthusiastically.

'How about the Mexican place? I can call them right now.'

'The one with the amazing margaritas?' someone else piped up.

'Exactly. Leave it to me.'

Soon they were gathering up their belongings, chatting away about what food they would order and how much fun they were going to have. Ana sneaked away to the bathroom and applied more lipstick, which matched her hair band and shoes. It was most inappropriate that she thought of Gabriel again as she smacked her lips together.

She'd caught him looking at her lips several times today. If he wanted a brief respite from his single dad routine, maybe she could offer to re-enact the dream he didn't even know she'd had, the one where her legs worked, as they often did in her dreams. She'd straddled him on the examination table and he'd held her tightly by the hips and made wild, passionate love to her so furiously, they'd broken the table. He'd run his fingers through her hair and told her she was beautiful and…well… It was a shame she'd woken up too soon from that one. Though not so soon that she hadn't flushed the next time she'd set eyes on him in real life…

'Come on, Ana! What are you doing in there?' Maria was calling her.

'Coming!' Tutting to her reflection, she realised she was hot under the collar. Of course, she would suggest nothing of the sort to Gabriel. Why would she go and ruin their friendship with something so transient as sex? He was just making her feel validated and important and people making her feel that way, especially hot guys, made her horny, that was all.

She would keep her hands, and her thoughts about her friend, to herself. Tonight, though, she decided as Gabriel shot her a look that sent her pulse racing, she *was* going to have some fun. She deserved it.

CHAPTER SIX

THE MEXICAN RESTAURANT in San Telmo was already bustling when their group arrived, and the waiter hurried to get them all seated. Ana was pleasantly surprised when Gabriel made a visible effort to place himself in the seat next to hers. His smouldering gaze threatened to set her cheeks on fire as he watched her while she pretended to read the menu. Did he feel her watching him too, as he pondered the burrito and fajita choices in front of him?

'It all looks delicious,' she said, licking her lips and tasting her lipstick. Had she put too much on? Why did she care? He was her *friend*. And he didn't have a clue how attracted she was to him right now. Or did he?

'What are you going to have?' he asked, leaning in, brushing her shoulder with his and wafting his manly, musky scent right up her nose. Ana cleared her throat. He might as well just have asked her if she wanted a naked massage for the effect his closeness was having on her.

When had this happened? Now she just couldn't ignore it. He also looked so handsome in his fitted white shirt and tailored navy trousers. His dark skin gleamed under the lighting, and she couldn't shake the burning need to get closer to him physically and emotionally. She'd been AWOL too long. The fact that he was a single dad with a whole other life just intrigued and enchanted her more now and, combined with her dream…no. She'd have to rein it in! They were working together, for goodness' sake.

'I… I'm… Maybe the chicken,' she managed around her parched throat, and he threw her a sideways smile.

'So you're only a part-time vegan, then?'

'I'm a carnival vegan; I told you.'

'A carnival non-carnivore?'

Suppressing a nervous laugh, she made to pick up her margarita just as the waiter placed a basket of corn cobs down in her path. 'Oh, shoot!' Her drink went flying. A gasp echoed around the table as the liquid pooled and settled in a slushy wet splodge on her shirt, rendering the left side of the white cotton totally see-through, right down to her blue lacy bra. Groaning, she went for the napkins just as Gabriel did.

'You're not having much luck with your drinks today,' he quipped, stopping just short of mopping her breast. For a second he looked more horrified than she did, but somehow, for reasons she couldn't explain other than her general mortification in this moment, she burst out laughing until the whole table was killing themselves.

'It's just a shirt!' Maria giggled, standing up so Anna could wheel her chair past. 'We've all seen worse.'

Gabriel stood up too, dropping the cloth napkin. He made as though he was about to help with her wheelchair, but she expertly manoeuvred herself past, throwing him a look to say, *thanks anyway*. She wasn't laughing any more by the time she reached the bathroom. Her shirt was soaked. Somehow she'd have to do her best to forget it, though; fun was on the agenda, and nothing was going to ruin this rare night out.

It was sweet that he still wanted to help her out after all this time, like he used to do at school in the months after her accident, back when she'd still been trying to work out how on earth she'd get through this thing called life when she couldn't even walk. He seemed to see she had worked it out by now but, back at the table, when his arm brushed hers again reaching for his own drink, she wasn't so quick to move away. At one point, she couldn't stop her fingers from reaching out to the corner of his mouth and wiping a tiny bit of red sauce away. He thanked her, chocolate eyes shining in the low lights, and in her mind he kissed her again, as he had done in her dream, as though it was just the two of them and they were on a date.

They'd never been on a date in real life. *And you never will*, she reminded herself. *Friends don't date!*

Somehow the atmosphere in the restaurant made her feel tipsy without having drunk much at all. Everyone in her small team seemed to be enjoying this reprieve from the stresses of the past week, and she allowed the sudden rush of pride that consumed her and almost brought a tear to her eye. OK, maybe she had drunk a little more than she'd thought.

'What are you thinking?' Gabriel whispered suddenly in her ear, causing a flurry of sparks to travel from her earlobe through to her belly. Her heart thundered like a racehorse on course to the moon as she concentrated on the heat radiating from his body in the small, bustling, candlelit space. Why was her throat constricting—because she hadn't been this close to him physically in years? Oh, gosh, did he feel it too—this growing whatever-it-was that she could almost reach out and grab from the air between them?

She still hadn't spoken. 'I was thinking how proud I am of everyone here,' she told him, putting down her margarita. No more drinks for her.

'And yourself, I hope.' He smiled softly. 'You should also be proud of yourself, Ana.'

He said it so sincerely that the tears really did threaten to fall this time. She released a breath, nodding slowly, focusing back on the flickering candle flame so as not to reveal how his proximity was making her feel. It was more than his good looks, it was the way he looked at her—as though he was taking in every single, miniscule detail, adding it to some sort of mental checklist, memorising ways to please her, help her or make her laugh.

Gabriel had always done this, she realised now. She'd just usually been annoyed by it more than flattered, growing up. She hadn't wanted to be noticed for a long time, in case all people saw was her disability.

The weight of his forearm touching hers as he leaned in to read the dessert menu, the physical nature of him, his presence, the way he looked, his skin, the way he smelled and his touch... Oh, boy. Neither of them had time for this...inconvenient attraction.

'Ana?'

'Yes?' She looked up, only to find her whole team, and the waiter, were looking at her expectantly. She cleared her throat, realising the scratch of the waiter's pen on his pad, his low baritone explaining the difference between the chocolate-

covered deep-fried specials and the clink of cut-
lery and glasses had all gone completely over
her head. She had been completely lost in Gabriel. No, no, no…this would have to stop. She
would eat her dessert and leave, she decided. Her
friend was…her friend. Wasn't that what she'd
told Maria? Why could she not just convince her
stupid brain to believe that was all she still saw
him as?

'Um, I'll just have the churros,' she said
quickly, hoping no one realised she hadn't even
been reading the menu.

The waiter huffed a sigh. 'I did just explain that
we don't have any churros left, ma'am.'

She lowered her head and muttered that she'd
have the sorbet. They had to have that, right?

Gabriel was smiling softly beside her. To her
surprise, he reached out to squeeze her hand
lightly. 'You're tired, huh?' he said now. 'I'm exhausted too. Big week.'

Ana blushed so deeply, she could feel it. How
embarrassing that he thought she was tired when
really she'd been totally distracted, completely
caught up in him, that was all. Gosh, if this crush
got any worse, people would start to see it…if
they hadn't already. 'Big week,' she agreed. 'And
thank you, by the way. I wouldn't have as many
reasons to feel so proud if you hadn't been at my
side all week. People love you.'

'I love…that they love me,' he said, knocking his knee to hers under the table. Their fingers entwined together over the table cloth for just a few seconds longer before he seemed to think better of it and let go. Her hand was instantly colder.

Maria was looking between them over her margarita even while she talked to Sandrine, their part-time physical therapist, and Ana forced herself to start a fresh conversation with someone else. Knowing that her gorgeous best friend believed in her dream as much as she did filled her with the kind of new-found hope for the future that had seemed somewhat impossible until now. She really could do anything. But this attraction had to be stomped out if they were to continue.

Wait a minute… Had he just been *flirting* with her, knocking her knee under the table, squeezing her hand?

Just then, Gabriel slid his chair back and got to his feet. Men and women, couples and friends all around the restaurant, turned from their tables as he clinked a fork to the side of his glass. Ana sat up taller, even though the sudden urge to shrink took hold. Oh no, what on earth was he going to say?

'Ladies and gentlemen, I'd like to raise a toast,' he said. 'To Dr Ana Mendez, who's been working so tirelessly for so long to make this dream come true. She's a true inspiration and I'm honoured to call her one of my friends.'

One of his...*friends*.

Ana sniffed, even as her stomach dropped. Of course, everyone knew they were friends; he was just seizing the chance to reiterate it. He raised his glass and everyone followed suit, clinking their glasses together, but Gabriel wasn't done.

'Her commitment and drive have always been nothing short of incredible, but this week... Wow...' He trailed off a moment and fixed her with a look of such pride and admiration that Ana felt the tears start to prickle persistently behind her eyes. The six familiar faces were smiling, nodding at her and to each other, celebrating her work and achievements. Maria was looking at her with admiration too, while Sandrine nodded in silent approval, but it was Gabriel's gaze that made the fizz begin under her skin. Yes, he'd drawn a line under their friendship, but his warmth was spreading through her, straight to her heart and on through to everywhere else. Her dream came flooding back all over again in full colour till it was all she could do not to lunge for him.

No. No, she would not let herself, or their friendship, down.

She would resist. He was a proud friend, an old friend, the best kind of friend. Quickly blinking away the tears before anyone at the table noticed, she drew a breath deep from her jittery lungs before raising her own glass. 'Thank you,' she said softly, feeling an unfamiliar surge of happiness mixed with helplessness take hold of her chest as their eyes met again. This was…too much.

'I should probably get going,' she said.

Gabriel arched his eyebrows and sat back in his chair with a sigh. 'I should go too…' he started, but no sooner were the words out of his mouth than Sandrine and Maria stopped him.

'Oh no, you don't, we're going dancing! Bueno Tango needs your moves, Gabriel.' Maria wiggled her shoulders. 'Yours too, Ana.'

Maria was a little tipsy, and so was Ana, if she was honest. The last thing she needed was to steer her chair into people's ankles on a dance floor. Not that she couldn't 'dance' in it, so to speak, but the thought of making a scene, doing anything else embarrassing in front of this team of people who respected her position, didn't sit right. Her drink was already splotched on her shirt, though thankfully her bra was no longer on display.

'Not tonight,' she said, throwing them an apologetic look at the same time as signalling for the bill. 'You guys go, though. Have a great time, and keep the receipt—it's on me.'

'You don't have to cover it all,' Gabriel whispered now, a frown on his handsome face. She found herself matching his expression.

'Yes, I do,' she said, removing her red head-band and placing it on again. Like her vision, it wasn't entirely straight. Why on earth would he think she wouldn't cover everything for her staff? Then she realised he probably wasn't used to this wealthier Ana who'd made a life for herself away from her overbearing family and could actually afford to treat the people she cared about.

'Well, it's very generous of you,' he said, and she shrugged. More than anything now, she just wanted to escape. If she couldn't have him as more than a friend and colleague, she would have to leave him here as a friend and a colleague. Sliding her shiny new business credit card onto the waiter's tray the second he approached with the bill, she turned to Gabriel.

'Are you staying?' she asked. Her heart was pounding in her ears, louder than the music.

He looked at her thoughtfully for what felt like an eternity then he crossed his arms. 'Do you *want* me to stay?'

Something shiny caught her eye and she gasped, reaching out for his wrist and pulling him closer. 'Your birthday bracelet! You still have this?'

He frowned in surprise. 'Why wouldn't I?'

Ana smiled now, a warmth spreading through her chest as she turned the silver bracelet over on his wrist, taking in the tiny horseshoe engraved into it for good luck. She'd worked hard at a Saturday job in order to pay for it, had chosen and wrapped it carefully and presented it to him for his sixteenth birthday. She couldn't believe he'd kept it.

'Your birthday was right before you were due to play that football match against the Boars, from the barrio over from ours.'

'They were mean.' He grinned now, watching her face. 'I needed that good luck.'

'You beat them, didn't you?'

'Yeah, we did!' He laughed. 'So, I guess it worked.'

'I remember you running to my house to tell me. Where did you find it?'

'What do you mean, where did I find it? I wear it all the time,' he said.

'Liar!' She made to swipe at him playfully and he batted her off until they were play-wrestling like the kids they'd been back then, when he'd raced to her house and recounted the whole story about how he'd scored the winning goal against all odds.

A cough came from across the table. Ana turned to find the girls still there, their mouths twitching.

'So, I suppose you two really aren't coming?' Sandrine said, glancing at Maria, who smirked back at her knowingly. After a few air-kisses, her team of tipsy people made its way out to join the throng of people heading towards Bueno Tango. Ana knew they were all probably talking about Gabriel and her now. Well, so what? They were just two people, reminiscing about silly childhood moments. He was just a friend...

Who had kept a good luck gift from her this whole time.

She looked down at her fingers, now intertwined with his on the table. How had that even happened? Wriggling them free, Ana was suddenly overcome with equal tiredness from the drinks, the long week and the sense that she was growing increasingly confused and out of her depth.

'I really should go,' she said.

Gabriel nodded, then put a hand on her shoulder that sent her heart into overdrive. 'I'll accompany you home, if you like?'

On the way past the restaurant's reception, Gabriel swiped something from a vase and held it behind his back. Out on the street, he produced a marigold, and held it out proudly to her. She laughed, feigning shock. 'Did you just steal that flower from the restaurant?'

'It's not stealing if it had your name on it,' he said, revealing the dimples she adored, and her breath hitched as he moved her hair aside. Slowly and intentionally, he placed the flower gently behind her ear and met her eyes. 'It suits you.'

Ana's heart raced as they made their way onto the moonlit streets. The night was balmy and busy with groups of friends talking excitedly, and couples whispering closely. She could literally feel an electric current pulsing between them, threatening to start a fire in the trees they passed as they walked. The stars above seemed like some timely reminder of their past, when the nights had stretched out in front of them and they'd had no plans, no responsibilities.

They walked and talked, about his shifts with Bruno and her time in Bariloche, but she still couldn't bring herself to ask if there had been anyone else after Ines. Instead she found herself remembering out loud the time when he had put her to bed drunk after graduation.

He just grinned. 'You're a funny drunk,' he said.

'I'm not drunk now,' she iterated. 'In case you think I am.'

'Just tipsy, right?'

'Exactly.' She pulled her chair to a stop and motioned to her front door. 'Well, this is me.'

He shoved his hands into his pockets. She couldn't read the slight smile on his lips as their eyes met and held. He should already be walking away, down the street to the small apartment he had near his parents' place, where he lived alone, except for when Javi and the dog visited. But he was still here with her, and her heart was pounding with anticipation; she was giddy as a schoolgirl. He was looking at her lips, just as she was looking at his. A thrill of excitement coursed through her body like a shockwave as Gabriel leaned closer, his warm breath tickling her skin.

He hovered for just a moment, running his fingers softly over the flower behind her ear before she reached for his shirt and urged him even closer. In that moment, she knew without a doubt that it was too late for either of them to turn back—way too late.

For a split second, the thought crossed her mind: *will this cost us our friendship*? But that thought was quickly silenced as Gabriel's lips touched hers then pressed down harder, engulfing all her senses. Waves of desire flew through her body like wild birds and left her breathless. All she wanted right now was to stay in this moment for ever and let the world fade away. Every fibre of her being wanted this man…

But then he pulled away and took a step back, seemingly gathering his thoughts. 'You know…' He groaned, almost under his breath, as her heart bucked. 'If I come inside with you, Ana, I don't think I'll be able to leave.'

Before she could think straight and let something as stupid as logic get in the way, she spun her chair back round to the street. 'Then I guess we're both going to your place,' she said.

CHAPTER SEVEN

ANA WATCHED AS Gabriel carefully measured out the lemongrass tea leaves and scooped them into two cups. Then he added hot water, stirring it slowly, almost seductively, in a circular motion. Ana felt her throat tighten as she looked at him in the bright kitchen light. It wasn't the tea she wanted. It was him she wanted, badly, but maybe he'd changed his mind about her and was about to soften the blow by reminding her they were friends.

She wanted to believe it would be beyond foolish to ruin a good thing. But this chemistry between them was like nothing she'd ever experienced before—it was thrilling and intoxicating, and even now she could feel a strange contraction in her heart muscles, pumping blood to places it hadn't been in a long time. That newly awake and fizzing part of her wanted to stay and explore what they could have, while the other part, the sensible part, knew damn well there'd be consequences if she did. But she was here, wasn't she?

The living area was cosy, from the open-plan kitchen to the soft textured couch and colourful rugs across the floor tiles. Ana rolled her chair towards the couch. Traces of his son were everywhere: a stack of toy cars in the corner, a drawing of a superhero tacked up on the wall, a pair of sneakers peeking out from under a chair. But she knew from their discussions that Javi was with Ines and her husband now, and Gabriel didn't have him till tomorrow. There would be no interruptions if she stayed, if he carried her in his arms up the carpet-clad staircase to his bedroom, if he laid her across the sheets and…

'Tea?'

Ana sucked in a breath quietly as he appeared behind her with a steaming cup. 'If it's too hot, let me know.'

'Thanks,' she mumbled as he cleared the sneakers away quickly. He sloshed a little of his tea as he kicked them towards the wall behind some fitness equipment and turned to her with a sheepish shrug. He was clearly nervous. So was she.

'Gabriel…' she said now, putting the tea down on the little glass coffee table and moving her chair closer. He put his cup down too and dropped onto the couch, rubbing his hands across his chin. 'Don't be nervous,' she told him, as she wheeled up closer, so close she could touch his knees with hers. He ran his gaze over her lips and his eyes grew even darker with hunger, and suddenly she knew he *definitely* wanted her. It was everything else he was nervous about: how to navigate her disability, her wheelchair, or how to treat her.

'I have to admit to you, I am a little nervous. Not because I don't want this…' he started.

'I know. It's OK.'

Ana watched him take a deep breath, as if steeling himself, and her heart felt as if it was going to burst right out of her chest as he took her hands and held them tight, then scooped her towards him. His hands felt cool against the back of her neck, and she inched even closer, letting him kiss her again. He had to know that she wanted the same thing he did, all of it. This longing—the heat, the passion, the connection— wasn't something they could just switch off. Even if this turned out to be a one-night-only event, she couldn't back out now. They just had to find a way to work around what she couldn't do so they could both enjoy the things she most definitely could.

It was always the hardest part; it had been the same with her ex in Bariloche. But this felt more intense, more meaningful, more important somehow. Every time Gabriel pulled his lips away and looked at her, his face told her he knew that too.

If only she had the words to tell him that she could handle herself and make sure he was comfortable in all scenarios but, right now, her breath was so taken away by the growing intensity of his kisses that she was starting to think she didn't need to say a word anyway. Before long she was as far out of her chair as she could get. If only she could break free, she thought; if only she could stand up, wrap her legs around him and feel all of him pressed against her.

His breath was hot and deliciously heavy on her neck, and a rush of electricity surged through her core and made her toes tingle. She could tell her chair didn't matter to him as he trailed kisses that made her shiver down to the crook of her shoulder. Then, suddenly, he scooped her up from her wheelchair in one strong motion and held her close against him, pressing more kisses to her lips. Ana felt herself melting into him. She groaned with mounting lust and pure animal desire as he made for the stairs with her in his arms, just as she'd imagined.

His bedroom was surprisingly neat and tidy, which she somehow managed to notice between kisses…passionate kisses, with so much heat, so much burning desire. 'I knew this would happen,' he said now, carrying her past the huge wooden dresser that took up the length of one wall. The shelves were lined with more books than she'd imagined he'd have. The walls were painted in shades of blue and grey, and the moon was a huge glowing bulb, spilling its pale light through the trees outside and giving everything an ethereal glow.

'You did, did you?'

'Yes, I kind of did, the moment I saw you again that first day when I jumped out of the ambulance.'

A king-sized bed sat in the middle of the room, covered in a soft navy duvet. Still holding her close, he flung it back to reveal crisp, white cotton sheets, before lowering her gently onto the bed.

'You're so beautiful,' he murmured, just as he'd done in her dream. Ana gasped, barely able to suppress her grin as Gabriel slowly leaned over her, bringing his face level with hers—close enough that she could feel each breath he took, hot with an anticipation that matched her own. She drew him into her lungs, reached up, cupped his face and felt herself melting even more as his deep-brown eyes locked onto hers.

'I'm going to be so careful with you,' he whispered. 'We can do this.'

Ana felt her heart swell, tears prickling her eyes all of a sudden. He was so kind, so gentle, with her. But she wanted more. 'You don't have to be gentle, or even a gentleman. I know you, remember?'

Her hands fumbled at her shirt and she undid

the buttons, gasping as he pulled off his own shirt, and in seconds they were naked, flesh to flesh. All fear disappeared as he stood before her naked, and she ran her tongue over her lips, seeing nothing but adoration and desire, and muscles she hadn't imagined he'd have. He worked out: she'd seen the treadmill and weights in the living room.

Ana felt her breath hitch as his hands moved down her body, exploring her curves and lingering on her skin. His touch was tender and caring, but in equal measures daring and passionate, making sure she was pleasured while still ensuring she wasn't in pain or uncomfortable.

'Are you OK?' he asked, his voice full of concern.

Ana nodded, feeling the warmth spread through her body. If only he knew she had never felt so loved, so wanted and desired before. She smiled at the rush of happiness that overtook her.

'Yes,' she told him, her voice soft and breathy. 'All I want is you.'

Gabriel's eyes never left her, his gaze turning her insides to liquid before he leaned in and kissed her again, his lips caressing hers as a wave of pleasure coursed through her body, her inhibitions melting away. She just might have discovered a new-found confidence in her body, a confidence she definitely hadn't felt before, despite trying all kinds of positions with her ex.

'Let's take it slow,' Gabriel said, pulling a condom from the drawer by the bed, his voice low and husky as he positioned himself over her again. She moaned in pleasure as he slid inside her, watching her face the whole time, his voice low and gritty, like broken glass in the moonlight, when he asked again if she felt OK. He studied her face intently, tracing his fingertips along the planes of her cheekbones and jaw as if memorising every feature. She assured him she was more than OK by rocking beneath him, every nerve lighting up as they found their rhythm. His eyes burned with such a fierce intensity that she felt as though tears might well up at any second. No, she would not cry, she told herself, squeezing her eyes shut and locking her arms around him.

She felt her heart racing as their bodies moved together, Gabriel's hands exploring her body, his touch arousing her in ways she never thought possible. 'How is this...us...?' she heard herself ask between kisses as his hands found her waist again, then trailed up and down her back, tangling into her hair as he pulled her in. She felt herself melting into his arms against his broad chest, her body trembling as their passion heightened.

Gabriel suddenly pulled away, his breathing

heavy. He looked at her, his eyes soft but so full of desire, it made her blood fizz. She felt him pause after a moment, his hands stilling on her body. He looked into her eyes, his gaze searching for something.

'What is it?' she asked, suddenly worried that he wasn't enjoying this as much as she was.

'You're amazing, in every way,' he told her, his voice still loaded with emotion as he swept her hair behind her ear. This time, she really did have to blink back a tear, which she somehow managed to hide by kissing him fiercely and hungrily till his movements sped up and slowed again in response to hers.

Ana realised she had never felt so safe, so cherished, before. Her body was in his hands and he was so aware of that, it was beautiful. She closed her eyes, feeling another surge of joy course through her body as she guided him into another position she knew would feel even more amazing. Every single thing he was doing felt incredible: his hands, his breath tickling her skin, all leaving her the sweetest sensation of being someone's everything, even if it couldn't last; even if this was the only time they'd ever do anything like this.

Gabriel's movements surged in intensity as they chased their mutual climax, and Ana decided that, unlike in some of her previous sexual encounters—when she'd perhaps felt a little embarrassed at times—she was going to make all the noise she felt like making and not hold back any involuntary shudders. As Gabriel collapsed beside her, their bodies exhausted from the exertion, she could barely keep from telling him how that had been far beyond anything she could have expected, better than in her dreams.

'Wow,' was all he said, and they laughed before he propped himself up on one elbow beside her. Gabriel looked down at her, taking in her features, trailing a finger across her bottom lip. His smile made the flock of butterflies re-emerge and whirl into a mad frenzy inside her chest before he kissed her forehead gently and slid out of bed.

Ana could feel the air between them still humming with electricity, even after he left the bedroom. When he came back, he was carrying water in two shiny blue glasses. She glugged hers back appreciatively. All that action had made her thirsty, and she remembered the tea they hadn't drunk going cold downstairs. Not that she ever wanted to leave this bed, now that she was finally in it. Soon, they both fell asleep, and for Ana dreams of Gabriel swirled round in her head and melted away all the doubts.

Morning came round, however, far too soon. She glanced at his bedside clock, which read six-fifteen. The birds were singing and Gabriel was still fast asleep. For a moment, she studied his sleeping frame: the contours of his muscles and limbs against the crisp white sheets; his darkly handsome face against the crumpled pillowcase.

This was the embarrassing part, she realised now. She could hardly just sneak out and let him have a well-deserved lie-in on a quiet Saturday morning, the way she would surely have done if she'd had the use of her legs. She would have to wake him up to help her get downstairs. Things were already going to be weird anyway, she supposed grimly, nudging him gently.

He stirred and his eyes fluttered open, and Ana prepared herself for a hint of regret on his face, some sign that he might regret putting their friendship on the line. But Gabriel just smiled at her softly, as if he couldn't believe his luck that she was still there. 'Good morning, you.'

Ana couldn't help but smile back, her heart stopping its heavy thud for a second in relief. He seemed to be genuinely happy to see her still there beside him in bed, as if she could be anywhere else. All the same, she was pretty sure they *both* knew this was the awkward 'morning after' moment, and at some point they would have to talk about it and what happened next.

Gabriel just sat up, yawning, and leaned against the headboard, stretching his arms behind him. She studied his broad chest, remembering how he'd cradled her so close to him before they'd fallen asleep. Would they ever do that again, or had it been a one-off? So many questions, but now…

Ana bit her lip nervously. 'I should go,' she said, holding the sheet around her now, slightly more self-conscious of her body in the morning light. He looked at her a moment before he seemed to realise what she was saying.

'Oh, right, yes…' He flung the sheets back quickly and scrambled for his clothes, and she watched in appreciation and amusement as he pulled his boxer briefs and trousers on so fast, he almost tumbled over.

'Sorry,' he said and she laughed. Somehow he'd lightened the mood again. He looked extra-cute in the morning light, eyelids still heavy as he dashed his hands through his tousled hair. She wanted more than anything to be able to tell him how much last night had meant to her, how much she cared about him, and how she'd never before felt so safe and cherished and adored. But maybe she'd come off as too needy, she decided. Still, she let her arms curl around him once he'd passed over her clothes and swept her up again into his arms.

When she finally left, he stood, shirtless, halfway behind the front door as she made her way back to the street. Her heart was doing crazy moves behind her ribs again as she kept on steering her chair away from him, putting more and more distance between them and their night of passion. Already she wanted to turn round and go straight back, but she didn't want to stay so long that it got any more awkward. All the 'what if?'s were piling up in her busy head already: what if he wished they hadn't done that? What if it *had* ruined their friendship for ever? What if…what if he didn't want to do it again?

CHAPTER EIGHT

'DON'T FORGET HIS JUMPER. He might need it,' Ines reminded Gabriel as Javi made to rush past them both from the house towards Gabriel's car. She kept one eye on her son the whole time, and her arms were crossed, as if she was physically re-straining herself from reaching out and making him stay with her.

'I have the jumper, and he'll be fine,' Gabriel said kindly, stepping back from Ines' doorstep. Nothing was going to ruin his good mood today. Not that that was entirely all to do with the fact he was spending the day with Javi. He could taste Ana on his lips and still see her face in his mind's eye, still feel her. What a night.

'What time will you be bringing him back?' Ines asked, catching him before he turned to the car, and handing him Javi's super-hero back-pack. No doubt she had already packed it with a ton more stuff that he already had for Javi at his place, but he was used to this pedantic packing by now. It was just Ines's way of showing motherly concern; he couldn't really blame her.

He told her he wasn't sure what time they'd be back from the wildlife park, but that he'd text her, and then he noticed Pedro's shadow through the pane of glass in the study door. Ines's husband hadn't emerged yet. Usually he came to the door to see Gabriel when he arrived to collect Javi.

'What's he working on?' he asked Ines. Ines looked away and crossed her arms.

'I don't know… Something.'

Gabriel knew that tone of voice. She had something on her mind. 'Is everything all right?' he asked, slinging Javi's pack onto his shoulder. Instincts primed, he watched her carefully as she studied her nails a second and blew air through her nose, sending her mass of black curls out around her slanted cheekbones. OK, so everything was not all right. In fact, it looked a lot as though he might have interrupted an argument or something, but it wasn't his place to bring it up.

'Bye, Pedro,' he called to the closed door. Pedro's shadow raised a hand from his chair but still he didn't get up.

Gabriel forgot about it as soon as they were in the car. He was already focused on thoughts of Ana again. She hadn't exactly left his head all morning but now he was wondering…would it be crazy and way too impulsive if he invited her on their day out today? She couldn't be spending all day working, it was too nice outside for that, and Javi would love it if she came. The wildlife park was suitable for wheelchairs, too.

Temaiken was one of his favourite places to explore with Javi. The wildlife sanctuary and conservation centre was home to a pretty impressive collection of habitats, and each one had been fastidiously designed to replicate the native environments of its furry, scaly, or feathered residents. He could already picture them all strolling through the lush, tropical rainforests. Maybe he would steal a kiss from Ana in a desert, or beside one of the ponds or waterfalls. Hell, he could at least ask her to come, right, even if he was getting ahead of himself? he thought as he drove.

Javi was jabbering to himself in the back seat as Gabriel pulled up outside Ana's place. Ines lived on the other side of Recoleto but he'd do a loop for Ana. Standing on her door step, he told his pounding heart to calm down, and it almost took the words from his mouth when she opened the door and looked up at him in surprise.

'Couldn't keep away from me, could you?' she said with a flushed smile, which he was sure he returned, though he was mildly distracted by another colourful headband and bright-blue sneakers that matched the pattern on her T-shirt.

'Javi's in the car. He was wondering if you'd

like to join us at the wildlife park?' he asked
hopefully. Ana studied him closely from her chair
and he wished he could read her mind. Was that a
trace of apprehension in her eyes? Was her heart
beating as hard as his? He wasn't quite sure he'd
ever felt this nervous on a woman's door step before; she was doing strange things to his insides,
even fully dressed.

'Javi wants me to come, huh?'

'Absolutely. Me, I don't want you to at all, but
I promised him I'd ask.'

Ana laughed softly and rolled her eyes. 'I had
a few things to do, you know, but…'

She let her words falter and trail off, then failed
to hide a smile behind her hair as she shook her
head. 'Let me just grab my bag.'

They chatted light-heartedly in the car, Ana's
wheelchair folded neatly in the back while she sat
beside Gabriel in the front. Even though he knew
she was making an effort to seem normal in front
of Javi, who was delighted she was joining them,
Gabriel knew she must be thinking the same kind
of things as him. He'd known last night, in the
restaurant, that if he walked her home he would
end up kissing her; and he'd known, when he'd
kissed her, that if he asked her back for tea they
wouldn't actually end up drinking any. He'd taken
a risk, putting their friendship on the line, but he

couldn't have helped it, even if he'd tried. Which he hadn't. Well, not very hard, anyway.

He reckoned, if he'd left it too long before initiating something like this, it might get even weirder. They still had to work together, at least for the next few days until she could find another locum.

The sun hung high in the clear Buenos Aires sky as he flashed their tickets and they walked through the entrance gates of Temaiken. The sound of gently flowing water filled his ears and just ahead the vibrant reds and greens of exotic birds squawking and preening in a giant aviary set the scene for the tropical gardens in one direction. A sign with a lion on it made Javi race in the other direction and Gabriel followed beside Ana's chair, careful not to try and help her.

She hated that. But she hadn't minded him carrying her up and down his stairs last night and, if he was honest, he'd loved that part the most. There'd been something far more intimate about her actually letting him help her, and care for her, than the act of sex itself.

'This place is really something, isn't it? I haven't been here in years,' Ana said, her eyes wide with amazement as Javi pointed in excitement at the lion enclosure.

His infectious enjoyment spread and soon they found themselves talking and laughing their way around the park, weaving in between other groups of friends and families and taking silly photos around the enclosures: of a llama with its tongue out, a goat chomping on a bale of hay and a snake curled around a branch in the glare of an orange bulb in the reptile house. Sometimes it was as if nothing had happened between them last night, as though they were still just platonic friends having a day out for old times' sake. But every now and then she would catch his eye and he'd feel it in his blood—something was different. An indelible line had been drawn through that friendship status and now he just wanted to kiss her again.

'It tickles!' Javi laughed as a huge red-and-brown-speckled butterfly landed on his outstretched palm.

'Hold still, very still,' Ana told him, grinning in wonder as she tried to take another photo on her phone. They were in the butterfly enclosure now, and the sweet scent of tropical flowers filled the air in the huge greenhouse. Javi was enchanted, reaching out to try and touch them as they fluttered by. He rarely managed; they were so fast they could barely even capture any on camera, though Ana was trying her best, to her credit.

'I remember what it was like to be that carefree,' she said with a small sigh as Javi ran up ahead of them after another butterfly. 'Running around…with you.' She turned to him now, and the sudden sadness in her eyes made him reach for her hand.

'Before your accident,' he said softly.

She nodded in silence, squeezing his fingers against the arm of her chair. 'Everything can change so quickly. You can't let any moments pass you by, Gabriel.'

Her eyes were fixed on Javi now, but when she flicked her gaze back to his he knew she was talking about them, too. Things had changed for *them* pretty much overnight. They hadn't let that moment pass them by, even though they both knew it would have long-reaching consequences.

He knelt in front of her quickly, taking both her hands in his. 'Are you all right, about what happened?' he asked, running his eyes over her mouth as she drew the corner of her bottom lip between her teeth.

'Papa, look!' Javi was calling him again.

'One sec, buddy!' Fixing his eyes on Ana, he ran a thumb over her knuckles and dared to lean closer. Suddenly he was suppressing the need to kiss clean away any doubts she might be having about how much last night had meant to him, because he could see them written all over her face. Filling his lungs, he stepped closer and leaned in towards her mouth. But Ana moved her head, causing his lips to find her cheek instead. He paused for a moment, struggling for equanimity amongst the bustle of the crowds before getting to his feet. She probably wished she hadn't come here with them now.

'We shouldn't,' she whispered, nodding towards Javi, as shame coursed through him. She was right, Javi was here—not that he thought his son would care, but if it got back to Ines that he was going around kissing women in front of him she might have something to say about it... She might think Gabriel was a bad influence on him, and use it as another excuse in her armoury to ask for full custody, if it came to it.

'Sorry, you're right,' he said, wondering now if she *was* just trying not to get too close to him in front of Javi, or if she actually regretted last night. Ana smiled wistfully, watching a giant Blue Morpho butterfly that had landed on her knee. It matched the shade of her shoes. For a few moments they let the silence envelop them, an awkwardness slowly settling between them with the butterflies. It was far too hot in here.

'You know, what happened between us doesn't have to change anything,' he said tightly, walking beside her towards Javi as the humid air closed in and the palms swept his shoulder, as if reminding him to stay away from her.

'I hope it doesn't,' she whispered back, shooting him another apprehensive glance. 'I really,

really value your friendship, Gabriel, I always have. I was perhaps a bit…forward.'

He nodded, feeling slightly offended and bruised despite himself. All he'd heard was a reiteration of that word: friendship. Maybe he had been building this up in his head into something it wasn't. This amazing woman had just been excited about the first week at the clinic going so well, and at being surrounded by so many people who admired her and were out to celebrate her achievements. They'd both just got swept up on a wave, and he told her so.

'It was still a great night—all of it, not just the end part,' he added, leaving room for her to agree with him.

Instead she was quiet. 'Are you OK?' she asked after a moment.

Was he? He would just have to be, wouldn't he? No point making a big deal out of it now.

'Of course. And I value what we have too, Ana; I always have done. Maybe we shouldn't have…'

'You're right, we got carried away,' she said quickly, though she wouldn't meet his eyes now. 'We shouldn't have done that, really. Friends don't sleep together.'

'Right.'

Awkward.

'But then, maybe it was always going to happen,' she continued thoughtfully. 'You know—

because we're friends. Sometimes you just have to see if it's going to work or…not.'

He opened his mouth to assure her he'd thought everything had worked pretty well—everything that mattered, anyway—but he closed his mouth quickly. He was probably putting his foot in it more with every word that came out. Now he wasn't quite sure *how* he felt. This was Ana and he would accept her in any way she needed him: as a friend, a colleague or a lover, even if it burned.

'It won't change anything if we don't let it,' she said, sticking out her hand. 'Let's shake on it now.'

Before he could take her hand, a monarch fluttered up and promptly landed on her outstretched hand. Ana stared at it, blinking. Then, just as fast as it had appeared, it flitted away again and she seemed to forget the attempted handshake.

This was still all a little awkward, he thought as they continued their walk. They leaned over the fence to see the ostriches with their big, round, gawky eyes and tiny heads; they hand-fed the pink piglets in the mini-farm and put Javi on a new dinosaur carousel that hadn't been here before. Ana was acting normal enough, but the whole time Javi was on the ride she was quiet, and she also kept pulling her gaze away from him and fixed it on something else…as if he couldn't feel her watching him anyway.

Gabriel watched the carousel spin under the blue sky and saw Javi's eyes light up when he climbed off and Ana handed him some candy floss they'd bought from the nearby stall. She batted Gabriel's hand away when he made to feed her a soft, pink fluffy piece straight from the bag— something anyone would do to a friend—which stung, but he pretended not to make a big deal of it. Last night had changed everything and they both knew it but, if she wasn't going to risk their friendship over a heated night together, then he certainly wasn't going to push for it. Yes, they had crossed a line, and he'd remember for ever the many different ways they'd crossed it, but if it was only going to happen once he would just have to put it behind him, exactly as *she* was.

'Can we go and watch the sea lion show?' Javi asked them now, his brown eyes gleaming. This really was his favourite place.

'If Ana wants to,' Gabriel said.

She nodded warmly. 'That sounds like a great idea,' she told his son, and Javi made to push her wheelchair in the direction of the sea lions. Gabriel was quick to pull him back.

'It doesn't work like that. Ana can do that on her own,' he told him.

Javi pouted. 'I know she can,' he said.

Ana was watching them. Then she leaned over and grinned at Javi. 'You know, maybe if you climb up on here with me, we can both race your dad to the sea lions?'

Gabriel looked at her in surprise. Was she seriously fine with that? She just shrugged and helped Javi up onto her lap. He couldn't help matching his son's infectious grin as Ana sped forward suddenly, holding Javi tight.

'Hey, not fair!' Gabriel yelled out, sprinting after them. Javi screamed with laughter as Ana wove around the people on the path, with him trying his best to catch them up. To be fair, he wasn't trying too hard; he wanted to let Javi think they were winning. By the time he caught them up outside the sea lion exhibition they were both high-fiving each other at beating him. He couldn't help feeling that Ana was even better with Javi than he'd thought. She had a natural way with him that suddenly made him all the more annoyed that he'd crossed that stupid line with her.

Now, instead of looking at her as his friend, as he would have done, he was looking at her as someone very important and influential, whom his son was already coming to like spending time with as much as he did. Women like her didn't come around very often—if ever. And who wouldn't want more than friendship with a woman like that?

CHAPTER NINE

THE SEA LIONS were putting on a great show. Ana had been able to position her chair on the end of the row with Gabriel to her left, and Javi two rows in front, closer to the feeding session action but where they could still see him. It was so nice, watching the little boy so happy and carefree. Just as she'd thought, Gabriel was a great father. He was better than great: his son adored him! She wished more than anything that she had the ability to lift Javi onto her shoulders and run around with him, as Gabriel had done at various points today. He was the kind of exemplary dad that didn't even realise how excellent he was.

'Woo-hoo, yes, get the fish, get that big one!' Javi was yelling now as the trainer by the huge blue swimming pool tossed another fish for the sea lion to catch and devour for its dinner. When it succeeded and dove into the pool, coming up close to the glass, as if to show off to the audience, Javi spun round to them, grinning from ear to ear. 'Did you see that, Papa, Ana?'

'We saw,' Gabriel assured him, throwing Ana a sideways glance. 'He likes you,' he said to her. 'But what's not to like?' he added next, almost to himself, before sighing and shaking his head. Ana swallowed. OK, so of course it wasn't going to be easy, being friends after….well…that. But she would have to try.

She'd had to come out with him today to see if their friendship could be rescued. What would she do if she'd messed it all up? Gabriel was important in her life! But the tension was palpable now. Why had she pulled away from that attempted kiss in the butterfly house in the first place? It was proof that maybe he didn't just want to be her friend…which sent her stomach flapping with more butterflies than the enclosure could've handled.

But it was more than Javi being there that had freaked her out. It was that she was scared of getting into something she couldn't get out of, or even something she didn't *want* to get out of! How could she possibly give Javi and him the attention they deserved? She was far too busy— she had only just opened the clinic. She'd worked her whole life for this chance to do something amazing on her own, make a name for herself and prove all the nay-sayers and mollycoddlers wrong. Romance was a big fat no. It would only get in the way.

Friendship was all she had time to offer anyone, and besides, this was Gabriel! He'd broken
her heart once without even knowing it; there
was no way she could go through that again if he
decided this wasn't worth pursuing for whatever
reason. They might have agreed that sex wouldn't
ruin their friendship, but it already had, and they
both knew it. It was imperative they get that back
on track, no matter what.

Ana swallowed as her arm brushed his and the
crowd let out another cheer for the fishy feeding
exhibit in front of them. Friendship…. It was just
a word to her now, a word that no longer held the
same meaning, not now he'd been inside her and
had treated her like the most special, important,
cherished person on the planet. Everything felt
so different now that she'd slept with him.

Gabriel's phone buzzed. Sliding it out of his
pocket, he started scowling at the screen. Ines:
she could read it from here. It was impossible not
to hear the one-sided conversation between them
as they started talking, though she kept her eyes
on Javi and the sea lions in front of them. The big,
clumsy, slippery creatures were full and happily-
fed, swimming around while the staff answered
the kids' curious questions.

'I still don't know what time we'll be back, yet,
Ines. No, he didn't need the jumper you packed,

it's been too warm. It's the swimming pool you can hear… We're watching the sea lions…'

Ana couldn't help notice how stiff his shoulders had become, just talking to Ines. It wasn't her business, whatever was going on between them as they co-parented Javi, but after last night she knew she would feel even more awkward if she ignored the elephant in the room altogether.

'Everything OK?' she asked when he hung up.

Gabriel forced a smile to his face and her heart twisted. 'Fine. That was Ines,' he said, as if Ana didn't already know. 'She just wanted to know when we'll be back.' He sighed deeply and she knew from the sound of it that he had a whole load of pent-up feelings on the matter.

'Sorry,' he apologised, pulling a face. 'It's not your problem, Ana.'

Ana chewed her lip a moment, looking at his hand, close enough to take and hold in her lap in empathy. She wanted to so badly, just as she'd wanted to kiss him again before she'd cruelly turned her cheek to him earlier in a moment of fear and doubt, but she didn't.

'It sounds like she struggles to let him out her sight,' she commented after a moment, as a sea lion honked in response to something resonating from the tannoy. An exotic bird demonstration, in ten minutes. That would be so lovely for Javi to see…

'She does struggle,' Gabriel admitted, dashing a hand over his hair. 'It's almost as if she doesn't trust me with him, or my parents. You know my parents—they love him. They'd do anything for him, but somehow it's never enough.'

'She's probably just concerned he might hurt himself on someone else's watch, like you are. Doesn't it come with the child-raising territory?' she reasoned. His nerves over telling him this were showing all over his face.

Gabriel shrugged, reaching an arm around the back of her chair, then abruptly removing it and sitting forward in his seat. 'I suppose it does. I just wish she would trust me a little more. He always has a great time with us, and he's perfectly safe. But I can't help thinking she's just counting down the days until she can ask for full custody.'

Ana turned to him fully, eyes wide. *What?* 'She wouldn't do that to you—you two aren't on bad terms, are you?'

'She's his mother and she's married. Sometimes I think Javi might *want* to just live with them permanently anyway. They can give him far more than I can.'

'Like what? You're his father! That counts for something. Might you just be worrying about things that won't ever happen?'

He nodded, contemplating her words, and her heart beat hard in her throat at how emotionally invested she suddenly was when she had been trying to tell herself that she shouldn't be. It wasn't anything she could help now, not after everything that had happened last night—not after he'd treated her with so much tenderness. But who was kind and tender to him, when he had doubts in his head like these? Gosh, she really had been a totally selfish friend to him. Before now, she'd only ever seen Gabriel as the strong one, the one *she* and everyone else could rely on. Gabriel had made a living doing everything for everyone else who needed him, but who took care of *his* needs? Who held his hand and told him when not to worry, and when to focus on what he wanted for a change, instead of what everyone else wanted from him?

'I'd better get him home after this,' he said now, glancing at her apologetically.

'Why? It's still early,' she said, suddenly annoyed on his behalf, and at herself too.

'Ines will just call me again in half an hour and ask me where he is. Trust me, it's better if we just get him home.'

'But he's having so much fun.'

As if on cue, Javi stood in his seat and clapped enthusiastically at one of the sea lions who'd caught another huge fish in its mouth. A kid in the front had thrown it.

'Papa, can we get a sea lion?' Javi called back to them.

'Sure.' Gabriel smirked. 'And let's just see how your dog reacts to that the next time he's with us.'

They continued to watch in silence. When he drove her home, she couldn't help feeling he was embarrassed at having shared so much with her. He didn't accept her offer to come inside with Javi, after he'd helped her back into her wheelchair with just as much care as he'd carried her up the stairs and laid her down on his bed last night.

'Are you sure? I have some great tea,' she teased, before she could remind herself not to.

His face remained expressionless as he turned back to the car, its engine still running. He was so distracted and probably still thinking about rushing back to Ines, who to all intents and purposes was in full control of Javi's *and* his lives.

'Better not,' he said, predictably.

'OK. Well, thank you for a great day. I had fun,' she said, looking up at his distant expression.

'So did I.' Gabriel seemed to be looking anywhere but into her eyes, and she could feel the connection severing right in front of her. 'I should get back to…'

'Yes, you should probably go.'

It was for the best, she thought as she closed the door after him and listened to the car drive away.

They'd both been confused and on a high after last night, and this was reality roaring back in to remind her not to get carried away. Gabriel—her *friend* Gabriel—had no space for her in his personal life; his hands were completely tied. He just didn't know how to say it after that one incredible night of passion they'd shared. Well, in that case, she would take the task off his hands and spare him the need. There was no way she was going to suggest any other close encounters, not even a cup of tea at her house, she decided.

Ana found herself staring unseeingly at the TV for the rest of the evening, knowing she should be doing something else, but completely unable to focus on anything. She had spent all her life keeping everyone—including him—at arm's length. Despite her growing real feelings for him all those years ago, she'd always just treated him platonically until she'd lost him altogether. Now, he had no space for her at all, no more than she had for him, realistically. Why then, if neither of them had the time or the space for this, did she feel as if something monumentally huge had just come crashing down around her? It would be better for her heart and whirring brain if she just stayed as far away from him as possible now, she decided. Except for at work—ugh. She could hardly avoid him there. She should step up her search for another locum.

* * *

The afternoon's rain only seemed to intensify the mood in the clinic's colourful consultation room as Ana passed Gabriel a file in preparation for their next patient. If only there was a way that he could ease this awful awkward atmosphere that had been hanging like a storm cloud over them all week.

'Who have we got next?' he asked as their fingers brushed across the papers.

'A kitchen victim,' she replied, moving away too quickly and making a thing out of straightening the pen holder on her desk, looking out at the rain pattering against the windows. 'He came in with his fiancé.'

Gabriel nodded, looking over the file. This weirdness between them was a living creature whispering from his shoulder whenever their sleeves or fingers met by accident, which happened a lot; how could it not in a place this size? She'd been looking for another locum since he'd started at the clinic, but so far there wasn't one with time to spare, and he knew despite this awkwardness that she still needed him. They were practically under each other's feet. He or she would make a concerted effort to pull away too fast whenever an accidental brush occurred, and look the other way, and it was getting kind of ridiculous now.

If only he hadn't said all that when they were watching the sea lions about Ines and his fears about her asking for full custody. Poor Ana had enough going on in her life just now—no wonder she'd backed away completely since then. They'd agreed their friendship wouldn't suffer but he couldn't help thinking it had been ruined even more now by his over-sharing. She probably thought he was a fool too, for bending over backwards for Ines and her demands, but what could he do? One foot wrong, and she might have another reason to get her lawyer involved in deciding where Javi lived permanently. That was something he couldn't compromise on, not for anything.

'Hello?' Maria opened the door slowly, peeking inside before, with a smile, sending their male patient in. His fiancé was close behind and the height difference in the two men made Gabriel bite back a smile despite himself.

The 'kitchen victim' was at least a foot shorter than his partner. He offered them both a slightly sheepish smile, cradling his burned hand against his chest as Ana introduced herself. His name was Davit and he spoke in English with an accent as he explained how grateful he was that they could see him at such short notice. He was Dutch, it emerged, the same as his tall, red-headed fiancé, Berend.

'Tell us what happened, Davit,' Gabriel said.

Davit flushed with embarrassment as he recounted the tale. 'I was trying to make a special lunch for Berend in the hostel kitchen—we're on vacation here. I was sautéing some vegetables and the pan just slipped from my hand. I tried to catch it, but...'

'But he forgot that hot pans are so hot,' Berend finished for him, pressing his hand to his fiancé's arm in sympathy, whilst also smiling ruefully at Ana.

Ana nodded sympathetically. 'Sometimes the most romantic gestures just don't work,' she said softly, reaching for Davit's arm at the same time as Gabriel. He caught her eye, as well as the double entendre, and almost tripped on her wheel. She spun away quickly, throwing him a look that was nothing short of annoyance, which he returned, before resuming his professional demeanour. Was everything going to be this difficult now? He would rather have his friend back than endure this weirdness between them.

'It's a second-degree burn with intact blistering,' Ana told Davit. 'Must be pretty painful, but nothing that won't heal up nicely as long as you don't get it wet.'

'And stay out of the kitchen,' Berend added, to which his partner play-slapped him and laughed, just before wincing in pain again.

Gabriel watched Ana work, as she wrapped the gauze carefully around the wound, her eyes devoid of the sparkle they'd held just last week, before their night together. It should've been obvious that working with her would be like this, though this was the first time she'd directed a slight his way. She must really regret that they'd put their friendship on the line...and annoyed that he'd had no time to stay behind after his shifts to try and talk to her properly.

That was his fault, he supposed. He'd been so intent on rushing to Javi, now that it was his week with him, and to relieve his parents of their grandparent duties once he was done with work. It seemed as if Ana had more on her mind than just him, anyway. But of course she did: she'd only recently opened her clinic!

There was also Ines to contend with. He was even more aware of having to keep things sweet with her than before, after she'd told him last weekend he'd returned Javi from the wildlife park later than she'd been expecting ...even though he'd texted her! She'd been distracted lately, so maybe she'd forgotten. He still thought it was unusual that Pedro hadn't left the study to see Javi and him off that day either, or when he'd brought the little boy back, but it wasn't his place to pry with personal questions.

Gabriel watched as Ana saw the bandaged-up

Davit and Berend out of the room after handing over a prescription for painkillers, and felt her eyes on him as she wheeled past, feeling the weight of his earlier mistake—clumsily impeding her wheelchair. Why did it suddenly feel as if he couldn't do anything right? Or maybe Ines was getting to him more than he realised.

He also still had his mother's invitation floating around in his head. Mama wanted Ana and her parents to come over to their place for dinner tonight. The menu was already all planned out. She was convinced it would be a fun reunion for them all now that Ana was back and the clinic was running smoothly. He hadn't quite managed to ask Ana to attend yet and time was running out. Maybe he should stop getting all up in his head about everything and just ask her, he thought. Their families were friends, after all, and what had happened between them shouldn't get in the way of that.

CHAPTER TEN

THE FLUORESCENT LIGHTS buzzed overhead as Gabriel ushered his mother Rosa, whom Ana had always called Mama Romero like everyone else, onto the examination table.

'Mama, what's happening?' he enquired in his most concerned tone, and Ana's heart flapped in her chest at the panic in his eyes. He probably hadn't expected his own mother to show up unannounced at the clinic—she had only called a few minutes ago when Gabriel had been seeing to Mr Acosta regarding the heart medication she'd prescribed for him.

'Thankfully you had a free appointment, and your father told me not to wait any longer,' the petite woman told him, clutching at her abdomen near her navel, the source of her discomfort.

'Your hernia again?' Ana heard him say.

'You did the right thing, Mama Romero, coming straight here,' Ana said reassuringly. Rosa's cheeks were flushed and her greying hair was damp from the rain outside.

As Gabriel offered her his arm for support, Ana felt a pang of guilt for being so cold with him lately, mostly out of self-preservation. She already regretted that snarky comment earlier today about romantic gestures going wrong. They had both made a mistake, blurring the lines of their friendship.

Only, she had been thinking about it ever since, letting his touch invade her dreams, craving more, and then firmly telling herself she shouldn't. The fact that he'd apparently been too busy even to talk to her about it any further had hit her harder than it should have, and she'd erected a wall, she supposed, as she'd always done whenever something threatened her equilibrium. He was back to being at arm's length, where nothing he said or did could affect her from ploughing forward as she always did.

Well, that had been her plan, anyway. It wasn't exactly working. And now here was his mother Rosa, in her own clinic, needing both of them.

'I had to leave Javi with your dad as he just got home from school…'

'Don't worry, he'll be OK,' Gabriel reassured her, getting her a cold glass of water from the tap and arranging a cushion behind her.

Rosa sighed, her voice laced with worry as Ana examined her, pressing gently on the skin around her belly and navel while Gabriel pressed a cold towel to her clammy head. 'The pain just started up again a few days ago, but it's getting worse. I was hoping it would go away on its own, but…'

Ana nodded empathetically as Gabriel gently took a blood sample and conducted a vitals examination. She supposed it must be tough, treating his mother like a patient all of a sudden. Her heart went out to him as she assisted, admiring his expertise and patient bedside manner, and how he managed to put his emotions aside, knowing his mother was sick and in pain. Her gaze lingered on his handsome face a moment longer than necessary, till he caught her and she had to look away again, annoyed with herself all over again.

'Will I need surgery?' Rosa asked them now, eyes wide.

Ana leaned in, keeping her voice soft and reassuring. 'We'll see about that. First I'll order some imaging tests and we'll have to see what the blood samples show.'

Gabriel chimed in, concern evident in his eyes. 'Have you experienced any other symptoms, Mama, like nausea?'

As Mama Romero described some occasional nausea, and Ana explained what she could do to curb it in future, Gabriel met her eyes again briefly, an unspoken understanding passing between them. They had both been making things awkward all week, but they were still irrefutably a team when it came to what really mattered.

They discussed Rosa's symptoms and, as they spoke, Ana couldn't help feeling more moved than she wanted to be by the love and respect the Romeros had for each other. Gabriel's family had always been so wonderful and warm; no wonder he had always wanted to base his life here amongst their love and support. Her own parents loved her too, of course, but it had always been easier to relate to Gabriel's, who had never smothered her the way hers had.

Ana performed the ultrasound, taking care not to apply too much extra pressure. Gabriel's eyes never left his mother, and she felt a pang of remorse suddenly at how she still shut her own mother out sometimes whenever she became overly protective and concerned. Ana had never enjoyed the close connection to her parents that Gabriel had forged with his—her fierce independence had seen to that. Their overbearing tendency to wrap her up in cotton wool had done nothing but make her want to run away, but they were all older now, and wiser. Maybe she should make more of an effort to show her parents that what they'd done for her had been appreciated, she thought…for the most part. Look where she was now!

'Thank you, Ana,' Rosa was saying now,

straightening out her clothes as Ana helped her sit up on the exam table. 'Look at you, both like this, making such a great team. It's so nice to see. And you've really made this place your own, Ana, I do love all the bright colours.'

'Thank you, Rosa.'

'Everyone loves the colours,' Gabriel said, looking directly at her. 'They're just so… Ana.'

Ana avoided his eyes once more as a vision of her clothing on his bedroom floor swept into her mind. How graceful he had made her feel the whole time, almost as if she had no disability at all. In fact, she'd felt perfect. He had treated her so wonderfully.

Stop it, brain!

Dutifully she wheeled the bulky ultrasound machine away again. The hernia had grown a little larger, according to her records, but all they could do at the moment was refer Rosa to a specialist and send her through to Sandrine to discuss how to manage and alleviate her discomfort with some small changes to her lifestyle.

'Did you decide on a time for tonight?' Rosa said to Gabriel as she straightened her light-pink cardigan. 'I mean, we can eat whenever you both like. But let me know when you think you'll arrive, so I can tell Juan and Martina.'

Ana frowned with her back to them. Juan and

Martina, her parents? She spun round to find Gabriel was pulling a face, as if he'd been busted.

'He didn't ask you yet, did he?' Rosa said with a harried sigh at Gabriel.

'To dinner, tonight? No, Rosa, he didn't,' Ana responded as he helped his mother towards the door a little more hurriedly than he should have. Her words had come out snippier than she'd intended them to, but why hadn't he asked her yet?

'I guess I didn't get round to it,' he explained with an insouciant shrug. 'We've both been so busy.'

Ana ordered her face not to display how utterly irked she was now. Maybe he didn't want to have dinner with them all and had been planning to wriggle out of it. Well, so much for that plan. Mama Romero had gone and dropped him in it—ha! Ana realised she was scowling at him now, and Gabriel was scowling back.

Rosa shook her head, lips pursed. 'You two! Always too busy,' she scolded them softly. 'Well, I think *both* of you deserve a night off with your families. You will come, it's an order.'

'I'd love to, thank you, Mama Romero,' Ana told her, picturing their old house and kitchen suddenly. The sink was always warm from the sun streaming in through the window. She remembered the moment she hadn't been able to reach the sink any more, when Gabriel had first brought her into his home in the wheelchair. There had been some happy times spent there as children, though, she and Gabriel running around the kitchen, getting in the way under the guise of helping to make dinner. There'd always been the warm, yeasty smell of baking bread, or the cinnamon scent of dark chocolate melting on cakes beside the stove. His grandmother would sing along to her favourite tunes, high-pitched and off-key. Baking on a Sunday was a weekly ritual at the Romeros'. Fridays were usually for family sit-downs.

'That's settled, then,' Rosa said brightly, smoothing down her dress one last time. 'We'll see you both at seven o'clock sharp at our house.' With that, she dropped a kiss on Gabriel's cheek and glanced back at them over her shoulder as she made her way back to reception. Rosa was the sweetest, Ana thought, watching her stop to admire the marigolds on the desk one more time. She'd always been so encouraging and kind, but she'd also always hinted that she'd love to see the two of them together some day, as more than friends. If only she knew…

No. She would never know, Ana decided. It would just make things even more awkward.

'So, were you going to invite me yourself?' she said to Gabriel when they were alone, unable to keep the shadow of a smile from her face now.

Gabriel dropped to the swivel chair and tapped

a pen on the desk, unbuttoning his coat at the top, as if he needed more air than the room could offer. Outside the rain was still pattering at the windows.

'Of course I was,' he said, meeting her gaze head on. 'OK, so maybe I waited because I wasn't sure you'd say yes.'

'Why wouldn't I say yes?' She tapped her nails on her knee, matching the rhythm of his pen, and refused to drop his gaze. It felt like a challenge.

'You know why, Ana.'

She feigned nonchalance. 'We said it wouldn't be weird between us.'

'Except it already is. You know it is.'

She screwed up her nose disparagingly. For a moment she almost caved in, almost moved closer and asked him outright if being friends was really such a good idea, and did he even remember how good the sex had been and how that was probably because they'd been friends first?

But then his phone rang, and he cringed, which meant it was Ines again.

'I should get this,' he said. She watched him walk to the window to talk and sighed to herself, pretending to check the schedule. Now she remembered exactly why it was pointless reminding him how good it had been between them. It wouldn't work, going forward, never. He had no time for her. His priority would always be Javi, as it should be. And hers was the clinic, as it should be. They were *both* too busy. Already the door was opening again, and Maria was sending in another patient.

The timing was always wrong for them, and it probably always would be. And now, not only did she have to find the strength to accept that, but she had to endure a whole dinner with both sets of parents present. How had her life suddenly got so complicated and confusing?

The house was just as she remembered it as she came to a stop outside and psyched herself up to go in. Just being here was bringing it all back. Gabriel's childhood home was a pale pink brick house of two levels, with a low roof of whitewashed slate and a funny-looking satellite array on top that his dad had erected some time in the early nineties for TV and radio and had left there even as more modern methods had been introduced. The antennae up there still turned in the wind sometimes, but surprisingly it had never fallen off.

'He'll never get rid of it. I've offered to remove it,' came a familiar voice behind her.

Gabriel stopped beside her chair and looked up at the roof.

'Remember when you carried me up there to watch the shooting stars?' she said, surprised at the way her pulse had quickened instantly the second she'd heard his voice.

'We're lucky nothing happened.' He grinned, and the way he looked at her made her stomach turn with a series of sparks that travelled up her arms. He meant it was lucky they hadn't fallen off the roof or something, but now she remembered how she had kind of wanted something to happen with him, back when they'd been teenagers, way before he'd met Ines.

'I'll help you up the steps,' he said as she wheeled her chair ahead of him, where he couldn't see her cheeks blush. The door was already swinging open, and Rosa was there, arms outstretched. Her parents would be here any minute. She had to let Gabriel help her inside, there was no other way.

First he lifted her gently from her chair, with the utmost care and attention. He carried her up the steps and held her in the doorway while his father—a tall, broad-shouldered man with a deep voice and friendly eyes like Gabriel's—brought her wheelchair past them, and she couldn't help filling her lungs with the scent of him. It was the musky cinnamon smell she had always associated with Gabriel.

It reminded her of a time when they'd been sixteen, and a group of friends had gone to Cerro Tres Picos for a weekend to camp in the forest.

Her parents would never have let her go with them unless Gabriel had convinced them he'd take care of her. And he had. He had carried her then, too, from the car to the campsite, where they'd sat out all night under the stars, and then from her chair to the tent, and she'd trusted him implicitly. He was the only guy she'd ever trusted to treat her so carefully, she thought with a pang.

Soon she was nestled in a pile of cushions, being handed a glass of wine. Inside the house was cosy despite its cool, tiled floors. The familiar kitchen just off the open lounge was still the same with yellow walls, peach-coloured floors and little tiles painted with pictures of tropical birds. The scent of empanadas filled the air.

She drew a deep breath and forced her face into a neutral expression as Gabriel sat close beside her. His eyes burned into her cheek every time she spoke or answered one of his father's questions. Rosa, thankfully feeling a lot better now, bustled away in the kitchen, humming to herself, clinking utensils, plates and glasses and occasionally calling out to his father for something she couldn't reach in the pantry. Ana had always loved this happy home. She was just starting to feel comfortable, regaling them with a story about a particularly funny encounter with a neighbour in Bariloche, when the doorbell rang.

In a flurry of greetings, Ana's parents were

ushered into the room. Her father looked as smart as usual in his ironed cream chinos, a crisp shirt and a brown leather belt he only wore for special occasions. Her mother had on her most elegant jeans, an embroidered blouse Ana had brought her back from Peru after a conference in Cusco a few years ago, and heeled sandals. They were very fashionable, and fashionably late, as usual. Ana let her mother kiss her cheeks, enduring it when she then wiped a lipstick smear from one and frowned at her choice of head scarf. She'd gone for a bright-blue one this evening, because Gabriel had commented on how much he'd liked it during the week, she realised now.

'It's so lovely to see you, Gabriel, and even nicer to see both of you together again. I've been hearing you're the angel of the clinic, Gabe.' Her mother cooed at him. Gabriel shot Ana a side-ways smirk behind his hand as he too endured a kiss to his cheek, whilst Ana continued wiping the lipstick from hers. 'Is it gone?' she whispered.

'It's all gone,' he assured her with a wink.

'Thanks.' Ana felt her cheeks flame. There was nothing worse than feeling reduced to a useless child again by her mother, especially in front of him.

'Let's eat!' Rosa enthused.

Right away, her father sprang into action, wanting to assist Ana with getting back into her wheelchair, as he'd always done. He was nimble for a man in his mid-sixties, but Gabriel was faster. 'I'll help her,' he insisted, holding out a hand to her. 'If Ana's OK with that.'

'Of course.' She smiled gratefully as he lifted her again with ease and helped her back into her chair. Despite the fact he'd left most of her mother's lipstick on his own cheek, she couldn't deny he was an angel at the clinic—a devilishly handsome one. Again she breathed his homely scent and let her arms loop around his shoulders, wishing the act could take longer than thirty seconds. This was the closest she had let herself get to him all week and she'd missed it. Of course, this was all for their parents' benefit, though, so they wouldn't pick up that anything was wrong.

Still, it was hard to miss the look Rosa and her mother gave them as Gabriel helped her gently back into her chair. They sat at the table before the feast that Rosa had prepared: empanadas filled with sautéed beef and vegetables; barbecued short ribs; a hearty, yellow-orange *locro* stew made with white hominy corn; and roasted sweet potatoes topped with criolla sauce, all served on colourful earthenware plates that Rosa had collected over the years from markets all over Argentina.

It became very obvious, suddenly, that their parents had all been speculating about them behind their backs. And the point of the dinner was probably not just to eat all this wonderful food together... Talk about awkward! As much as they might want her to give them something to talk about, she and Gabriel would never be more than friends, and she was starting to think they both knew it. Ana suddenly couldn't wait to get out of there.

CHAPTER ELEVEN

GABRIEL TOOK THE last mouthful of his barbecued short ribs smothered in chimichurri sauce and caught Ana's mother looking between them with interest. She hadn't stopped with these questioning looks for the last hour and a half. While he and Ana were certainly giving off no hint of what had happened between them, he could tell they were all on the edge of their seats, waiting to hear that they were more than friends and colleagues.

'So, Gabriel, any new love in your life lately?' The question somehow still caught him off-guard. Ana's mother was looking at him intently. 'I haven't seen Javi in a while; is he still living at Ines's place?'

OK, so she'd decided just to come out with all the personal questions at once. He put his fork down and sat back in his chair but, before he could speak, Ana cut in. 'Mama, you don't have to put Gabriel on the spot, you know. There is such a thing as keeping your business private.'

Her mother pretended to pout. 'I was only asking, *cariño*. We're all family here, are we not?'

Ana's father seemed to be trying his best not to laugh at the situation. Gabriel couldn't tell if it was out of nerves or amusement, but his own parents had their mouths hidden by their wine glasses.

'Everything is fine, thank you, Mrs Mendez. Yes, Javi is with Ines a lot. And, well, I don't have much time for romance at the moment.'

Even as he said it, he could feel the air thicken as Ana tensed beside him. He cleared his throat, reached for the wine, filling their glasses, and switched the conversation to the weather, not wanting to cause any more trouble for Ana than he already had. However, before he could even put the cork back into the bottle, Ana's father cut in with a question of his own.

'Ana, are *you* all right? Is there anything we can do to help? You seem tense. Your mother and I were wondering if you need us to come help clean, or cook, or anything while you're at the clinic. We'd be happy to be more involved, now you're back and so busy.'

His offer was gentle and more than kind, as far as Gabriel was concerned, but Ana sat up even straighter in her chair and glared at them both, her eyes flashing with anger and frustration. 'No,' she answered gruffly. 'I don't need your help, thank you. I *don't* need anything. How many more times do I—?'

'What she means,' Gabriel cut in quickly, reaching out and placing a hand on her arm before she all but exploded, 'Is that she's perfectly capable of managing all that. Well, she can't cook, obviously. She over-cooks every vegetable to the point of mush, always has, but she has the right restaurants on speed dial, right, Ana?'

Ana chewed her lip, tapping her nails on the table while their parents all shuffled awkwardly. She had inherited her mother's eyebrows, which were thick and black, and they arched to his favourite blue head scarf the second he nudged her under the table.

'I do—all of the right restaurants—they know me,' she confirmed quickly, throwing him a sideways look that wasn't quite a smile, but wasn't a simmering volcano of a glare either. 'Sorry, Mama, Papa; I'm just…tired.'

'That's OK, *mija*,' Gabriel's mother soothed, starting to gather up empty plates. 'It's important work you do, both of you.'

Gabriel smiled reassuringly at Ana's parents, trying to project a calm confidence, and changed the subject to Javi's dog, Savio, and the upcoming 'pawrents' day' in a few days' time at Parca 3 de Febrero, near Javi's school. He told them about the smart terrier mix Pedro had rescued, who basically stuck to Javi's side wherever he was, and the tricks he and Javi had been teaching him. Ana stayed quiet and withdrawn.

He knew she was counting down the minutes until she could leave. Her parents had always wound her up, simply by loving her and caring about her. But he had to put himself in her shoes. She was doing more than fine on her own. She really didn't need them worrying so much about her any more. It must have felt suffocating, and only made her want to separate herself more out of defiance. Did she even need *him*? he thought, realising he was nervously turning his silver bracelet around on his wrist, and that she was watching. The thought that she might not need him any more than she needed her parents interfering in her life or standing up for her didn't sit right. OK, so the clinic was different—she needed him there—but was that enough?

Gabriel's jaw clenched and a familiar, prickling heat rose up his neck, just imagining the day she might find someone else to care for her. Someone less complicated than him, with more to offer her than he ever could. He already knew he'd have issues with that person. Deep down in his bones, there would always be a primal impulse to take care of Ana.

On the way home they took a detour. Gabriel walked slowly besides Ana's wheelchair along

the winding paths of the cemetery, smiling a little at how tired she looked as she rested her head
back against the chair and came to a stop at her
grandfather's grave.

'Thanks for walking me home,' she said on a
sigh.

'I wanted to.' He'd been here lots of times to lay
flowers on her behalf while she'd been away—
not that she knew—but he hadn't been here with
her in years. It was oddly peaceful in the moonlight—not spooky or eerie in the slightest—and
somehow it calmed his racing thoughts from earlier.

A few streetlights dotted the grounds and illuminated their path as they said their respects and
moved on. Ana didn't say much but, when Gabriel
finally stopped at one of the larger monuments
to study the inscription on a couple's gravestone,
she spoke softly.

'Imagine loving someone so much that you're
actually buried next to them when you die.'

He nodded slowly, raising his eyebrows at her,
and said nothing. *Imagine.*

'Thank you for this evening,' she said now,
with more than a hint of sadness in her voice.
She paused for a moment, adjusting the tie on her
headscarf, and added, 'And for defusing that situation with my parents. I'm not so good at dealing
with…all that.'

Gabriel nodded gently again and turned to face her, dropping to his knees. 'They love you, you know.'

'I know,' she said, studying his eyes. He was unsure what else to say in the moment, but looking at her now, wanting to sweep her up in his arms again but knowing he shouldn't, was killing him.

'Gabriel…' she started, her eyes weary but also determined, as if she was trying to make a decision that might have far-reaching consequences if she chose wrongly. But he was already leaning in, already cupping her face, and she was responding. He felt an explosion of emotion as his lips met hers, a deep warmth that seemed to travel right through him, radiating from his legs, arms and hands to his heart, till all he could feel was her. She was the total opposite of every other woman he'd been with, and her disability had nothing to do with it, he realised with a groan against her lips. She had a rebellious streak, and an independence that only he seemed to be able to break through to the soft, vulnerable woman inside.

Ana's hands moved up to wrap round the back of his neck as he deepened the kiss and Gabriel's heart raced in his chest as his breathing grew shallow with desire. She made him feel alive and *needed.* Even when her indefatigable ambition and drive for success blinded her to what really mattered, he saw how much she needed him emotionally, more than physically. Ines hadn't needed him at all. In fact, they'd had nothing in common besides one night that had given them both the greatest gift they'd never asked for.

'I like kissing you way too much,' he murmured against her mouth as the trees whispered overhead. This sense of being needed was something he hadn't felt for a long time. Now that Pedro was on the scene, filling his shoes, even Javi didn't seem to need him as much any more.

Nope, don't think about that now.

He felt her mouth part against his again and it made him forget all his insecurities. He focused only on the feel of her skin, soft yet firm beneath his fingers, and the way her lips moved so perfectly with his, just picking up where they'd left off.

Ana sighed against his mouth as he pulled away to look into her eyes. They were heavy with emotion now, but she smiled softly and nodded towards the exit. 'Walk me back?'

That kiss, Ana thought as they entered her apartment. Well, so much for trying to be friends. It had felt as natural as breathing to kiss him back.

It was dark inside. Flicking on the lights, she spotted some dishes still piled in the sink ahead of her in the kitchen. Thinking better of it, she flicked them off again, leaving on just one that lit a less embarrassing pathway up the stairs. That kiss had rendered her powerless to resist him and, even if she had to be brazen about it, or regretted it afterwards, she wasn't just going to stop there.

'Let me,' he said now, as if reading her mind. He motioned to the stairs, then swept her up in his arms again, heavily nudging the front door closed behind him with his foot in a dramatic statement of his intentions.

A chair lift had been installed to help with this part, but why let technicalities get in the way of romance? Suppressing a giggle, she let Gabriel carry her; he was good at it by now, and she enjoyed the way he swept her up with less care this time, letting passion override the need to treat her carefully.

When he lowered her onto the bed this time, she didn't even care about what she might look like, free from her chair and unable to move very much below her waist. It didn't mean she couldn't feel. Contrary to what a lot of people thought, she could still feel everything a man might do to her, and as her nervous giggles dissipated she found she was tingling in places that she'd been longing to feel tingly in since their last encounter. Oh…gosh.

'Oh, Gabe…'

Ana closed her eyes and melted into him, giving in to all the feelings flooding through her as Gabriel explored every inch of her body with his hands and tongue, lips and teeth. He was more than happy to help her. He seemed to move intuitively after just a few minutes, as if he'd been paying close attention before, memorising what made her most comfortable, which positions meant they could go further and deeper.

Kissing him, making love to him in her bed, was everything she'd been replaying in her head since they'd made love the first time, and more. How could she even have tried to forget the way he'd made her feel—as if everything else just melted away?

'You feel so good,' he mumbled against her into her hair, pressing deeper. The deeper he went, the more she wanted.

She was starting to need him. It had been beyond sexy, the way he'd been with her parents— softly reminding them what they should already know about her, without the need for an altercation. His gentle, calming energy and easy-going nature was a balm to her stressful reality, so to hell with feeling insecure or needy. To hell with pushing him away.

Soon, they were both breathless with exhaustion, falling apart with stars in their eyes, letting out a laugh in awe as they lay side by side on their backs.

'We should probably talk about this,' he said after a moment, lightly tracing the curve of her waist with one hand while his other arm lay protectively across her body. He seemed to take a breath before speaking and Ana couldn't help but wonder if he felt the same way that she did—as if they were on the edge of something beautiful and terrifying at the same time.

'I don't want to,' she told him quickly, not wanting to break the spell.

'Really?'

'Really. We know all the reasons this shouldn't work, Gabriel…'

'But it does work,' he said under his breath.

She sighed softly, nodding a silent acknowledgement.

There were no words that would help this thing make any more or less sense. They had something incredible that seemed to run deeper the more she tried to deny it. So maybe it was time just to stop denying it, she decided.

CHAPTER TWELVE

ANA PAUSED IN the clinic's doorway. The rain was picking up, not that it could dampen her mood in the slightest. No sooner had she wheeled her chair outside for a short lunch break than someone took her umbrella clean from her hands.

'A lady should never have to hold her own umbrella,' Gabriel said, appearing from nowhere and flipping it open over her head. Laughing, and feeling the familiar thrill of anticipation as he took her other hand, Ana followed his lead down the street and around the corner into the park, while he sheltered her from the rain all the way.

The last few days had started to blur for Ana. While Gabriel had started working with Bruno again this week, he'd still managed to put in a couple of shifts at the clinic as well. The droplets picked up in intensity, smacking hard at the ground and shaking the leaves in the trees all around them, but Gabriel didn't seem fazed, and at this point Ana knew she'd go anywhere with him. Well, within reason—she had a line-up of patients to see in less than thirty minutes, and so did he.

'You're early for your shift,' she said now, pulling out a bag of the tiny, delicious home-made empanadas Rosa had brought with her to her check-up this morning and offering him one.

'I was hoping to catch you at lunch,' he said, taking a bite and motioning her further into the park, where they stopped under her favourite tree, watching the rain.

'What is it?' she asked, suddenly suspicious. Things had been going so well lately, both with him and with work, and she had barely given another thought to the fact that they'd put their friendship on the line to pursue this. Was he having doubts now? The thought made her heart start to thump.

'Javi wants to know if you'll come to the 'pawrents' day' thing at the park,' he said, looking at her sideways. Between bites of his snack, he explained how Javi really wanted her to demonstrate the trick they'd been practising. Savio had learned to leap onto her lap in the wheelchair on command, as well as how to retrieve items from the fridge and bring them to her. Ana was pretty proud of her part in all this over the last few days, and spending more time with Javi as well as Gabriel and the dog had started to feel like a lot of fun. She'd never been part of a unit like this before.

'It won't be the same if you don't come,' he said.

'No pressure, then.' She smiled, while her heart continued its thudding, this time with joy and disbelief that, somehow, all of this was happening to her.

'I know it's happening when the clinic is open, but Ebony can cover now.'

Ebony was the part-time locum Ana had finally found who was able to cover whenever Gabriel's shifts with Bruno clashed with the clinic's.

'How do you know she can cover for us?'

'I already asked her.' Spinning her chair round so she was facing him, he bent to kiss her under the umbrella. Ana couldn't help the burst of laughter erupting from her throat as she tousled his hair, and the growing intensity of his kiss brought a soft moan to her throat. Soon her lunch was forgotten and they were feasting on each other in the rain.

It was so hot, kissing in the rain. So was the way she completely forgot where they were whenever she was with him, as if she were a teenager again. Wherever they were, her whole body felt filled with a sense of longing, but also total security, the likes of which she'd never asked for and hadn't known she'd needed. But how nice it was that he provided it anyway.

Come to think of it, she thought now, running her hand up and down his shoulder, admiring the feel of his impressive muscles, Gabriel was more emotionally available than anyone she'd ever dated. Yes, sometimes he still got waylaid by Ines and her demands, but it was nothing they hadn't been able to handle up to now.

'I'll come,' she told him quietly, breaking away for a second and gazing up at him as he stood tall.

He feigned shock. 'Already?'

'To the pawrents' day with you and Javi!' Ana pretended to slap him but he dodged her and took the umbrella with him, making her call out, laughing. Quickly he resumed his protective position over her and kissed her again, even more passionately than the last time. They were only forced to break apart when a lump of bread landed at Gabriel's feet. They stared at a cheeky bird, who pecked at the ground around her chair as if she was entirely in its way, and they turned to find a grumpy-looking old woman in a long red raincoat staring at them, shaking her head under a giant umbrella.

Quickly the woman deposited the rest of the bread on the ground and a flock of pigeons descended from the sky, momentarily blocking her from their view.

'Let's go!' Ana cried, still giggling as she sped back the way they'd come before the woman could chastise them again. Gabriel made pace with the umbrella close behind her.

'Why are you so wet?' Maria asked when they pushed their way back into the clinic.

'It's raining, Maria, that's what happens,' Gabriel quipped, winking at her as he pulled his white coat on and threw Ana hers.

Maria took her arm as she went to roll past and leaned down to her. 'Is everything OK?'

Ana's eyes were still on Gabriel's firm backside as he disappeared into the consultation room, but she drew them away quickly. 'Mm-hmm,' she mumbled. 'Why?'

Maria just frowned, as if deciphering all the things Ana's flaming cheeks must've been hinting at. 'Well, your mother was just in here. She said she's worried about you...you haven't been answering her calls.'

'Oh. Well... I had my phone on silent for lunch,' Ana replied heavily, yanking her phone from her pocket. Sure enough, there they were: six missed calls from her mother. Her heart sank on the spot. Why did she always feel like an incapable child the second one of her parents did this to her? Surely one call was enough, unless... unless something bad had really happened.

Feeling guilty, she called her mother back, following Gabriel into the consultation room. His eyes never left her face as she spoke, and she was quite sure the mounting shame she felt was evident.

'She wants to know if she can cook for me tonight, and you and Javi too. All of us,' she explained when she hung up.

Gabriel perched on the desk, smirking.

'What?'

'I told you—they just love you. You're always so defensive.'

'Can you blame me?' She huffed, although he was right, she supposed. 'It's just, every time they call, I assume they're going to offer to help me do something I can do perfectly well by myself.'

'I know. We all know how much you're capable of doing,' he said, his voice turning low and gruff and ten times sexier as he scooped her out of her chair and held her close against his chest, running his thumb along her lip. 'It's not like *I* can forget *exactly* what you're capable of doing.'

'Very funny,' she said, clutching his shoulders and marvelling at how her raised hackles seemed to calm instantly under his kisses. 'So, can you come?'

'What, now?' he teased, nibbling her ear.

She thwacked his shoulder. 'Stop it!'

'Can't. You're too sexy.'

Sighing, she ran her tongue along his lower lip, forgetting where she was again until…a knock on the door.

Gabriel swiftly placed her back into her chair and almost flew to the other end of the room, smoothing out his coat. He was pretending to study a file when there in the doorway, alongside Maria's, was a face she recognised. Ana felt her eyes bulge cartoon-style at the long red raincoat, before quickly regaining her composure. The elderly woman from the park… Of *course* it would be that particular woman who had just seen them kissing in the rain!

Gabriel adjusted his coat again in an effort to resume normality as Ana ushered their patient to the table, introducing herself. Ana's face was flushed, her lips slightly swollen. It was obvious they hadn't really stopped kissing till just now. He almost wanted to laugh, but he knew it wasn't particularly funny. The woman must think them both entirely unprofessional.

'You have pain in the stomach area? When did it start?'

Ana was examining her now, trying not to meet his eyes, although as she spoke the woman, whose name was Edith, kept flashing her cynical gaze between them, as if she really didn't trust them.

Ana cleared her throat and told them both she suspected it could be Edith's gallbladder.

'We need to do some tests to confirm my suspicions,' she said in her usual gentle but authoritative tone. Gabriel recognised this tone as a sign that she was struggling internally to feel the way she wanted everyone to believe she felt, when in truth she felt the exact opposite. Her mother had got to her, even without offering to do anything besides cook dinner, and now this. Maybe he shouldn't be kissing her in the clinic. As if he could help himself!

'First we'll do a physical examination, then Ana will run an ultrasound of your abdomen,' he said, grabbing his pen light and moving into position, brushing Ana's sleeve accidentally with his as he shone it into Edith's eyes.

'No sign of jaundice, no other signs of infection,' he said next, realising Ana had pulled away a little too fast and wheeled to the other side of the table where they couldn't touch, even if they tried. 'We'll also want to take a blood sample to check for certain enzymes. Anything that may suggest inflammation or blockages, Edith.'

Edith simply nodded. With her raincoat now dripping from a nearby chair, she was turning something that was tucked just behind the collar of her blouse, studying each of them as though they were detailed paintings on a gallery wall.

172 DARING TO FALL FOR THE SINGLE DAD

He stood taller under her scrutiny, but Ana was growing increasingly flustered and trying not to show it.

As reassuringly as he could, Gabriel continued his explanation as he inserted an IV line into Edith's arm and then watched as Ana injected a mild sedative into it. 'This will make you a lot more comfortable during the tests,' he told her, noticing Ana's hands were slightly shaking.

'Doctor,' he said quickly. 'Would you mind getting Edith some water? She needs to stay hydrated.'

Ana looked at him gratefully and rolled her chair to the sink. The woman seemed oblivious to the tube in her arm. Her gaze stayed fixed on Ana the whole time, before she interrupted Gabriel mid-speech and asked, 'Are you two married?'

Gabriel bit back a laugh. Then he saw what Edith was fiddling with behind her blouse collar. Around her neck a golden chain glinted importantly under the clinic lights. Fixed to that, currently getting his bare torso rubbed in devout adoration, was a pendant of Jesus.

'We're not married...yet...but we're planning on it,' he said quickly, forcing a smile to his face as Ana spun round in surprise, almost spilling the water. Eyebrows raised, he nodded subtly towards the pendant. Luckily Ana caught on.

'Forgive us for what you saw earlier, in the park,' she muttered.

'We're just deeply in love,' Gabriel followed, unable to stop the way his heart felt as if it was pumping an extra pint of blood around his body, lighting up his nerve-endings as he said it.

It was kind of strange, saying it out loud. He had never said it till now. He wasn't completely sure if he even felt it. He was still getting his head around the change in their relationship—enjoying it, loving the invites that were now coming in for both himself, Ana and Javi, even though Ines would of course have a say about dinner tonight at the Mendezes' place, seeing as it wasn't technically supposed to be his night with Javi.

For the most part he was still breathing it all in, loving the way Ana's mere touch sent electricity running through his veins. Of course what he felt was love. What else could it be? It had a wonderful ring to it, too. He should say it more often, say exactly what he felt. Life was short and the passion he felt even being in the same room as Ana was unprecedented. He would have shouted from the rooftops if he could have, from that stupid antenna his dad wouldn't take down, how proud he was to be with a woman like…

Oh. Hell.

Ana and Edith were both staring at him.

He'd gone off inside his own head again.

'I'll wait outside, doctor,' he told her quickly, leaving the room. Minutes later, after Edith was gone, he stepped back in to apologise.

'That wasn't ideal...' he started, but Ana drew a deep breath. There was no way to interpret her expression at all. It seemed to shut down and turn cold right in front of him. Then, to his horror, she gathered her clipboard abruptly, excused herself and left the room.

CHAPTER THIRTEEN

To Gabriel's surprise, Ines happily agreed to let him have Javi for the evening. She even drove him to his place herself, though left quickly, without even exiting the car.

'I need him back by nine p.m.!'

'OK.' Gabriel watched her go, scratching his head. Something wasn't right with her, and it hadn't been quite right for a while, but he couldn't put his finger on it. She'd given him Javi's usual bedtime curfew but she hadn't asked much about their plans for tonight, nor given him an extra set of socks for Javi, as usual.

'Are we going to Ana's?' Javi said now, as he led him down the street under the lamps.

'We're having dinner at Ana's parents',' he explained, trying to ignore another bout of dread that had been overshadowing his mood ever since he'd opened his big mouth in front of Edith this afternoon about being in love with Ana. She had been distant with him ever since. Whether he was still welcome for dinner or not in her eyes wasn't clear, but her mother had asked him personally in a text message, and he could hardly say no to Mrs Mendez. Besides he'd already cleared it with Ines.

The rain had dried up now, and they sat out on the deck, candles and fairy lights flickering across the big courtyard the Mendezes shared with their neighbours. He hadn't been aware till now that his parents had been invited too, but soon the Romeros were joining the rest of them around the table. One big, happy family, he thought in a moment of contentment, even though things were still somewhat strained between himself and Ana.

'Are we OK?' he asked her quietly, catching her arm as she went to pour him sweet, cold tea from a pitcher. 'You've been very careful not to talk to me since I said…that.'

She paused in her chair, and that cool look claimed her eyes again. '*That* what—that we're *deeply in love*?'

Gabriel's next words dried up in his throat. He got the distinct impression suddenly that he shouldn't have said it, even to appease an old woman's religious views.

'She wasn't happy that she caught us kissing in public when we're not married,' he explained in a hush, as if she didn't already know why he'd done it.

'I know that. That's not the point,' she snapped.

'We shouldn't have been so obvious at the clinic, Gabriel. We shouldn't be doing anything at all besides work! I've worked so hard for this opportunity and I need to be taken seriously.'

Her voice caught on the last few words and Gabriel took her hand.

'Ana. You know I wouldn't do anything that purposefully threatens your integrity, or anything you've worked for. You *know* that.'

'Well, you already did,' she said.

He felt himself stiffen. 'We both did.'

'Fair enough. But it has to stop now.'

'What do you mean, "stop"?' Gabriel clamped his mouth shut. He could feel their mothers' eyes on them now and he retracted his hand, realising his passion had completely consumed him yet again. He was about to demand she meet him out front so they could talk alone, but Javi let out a squeal from where Ana's father was teaching him to spear sausages over at the grill. 'Look, Papa!'

When he turned back, his mother had taken Ana hostage with another conversation at the end of the table. Their intermittent piercing glances burned into his cheeks as they talked.

Annoyed, he scowled into his drink.

OK, so she was worried about looking unprofessional—understood. She had indeed worked very hard for the clinic, to get where she was, and she already had a thing about needing to prove herself. Maybe he should have been more careful in what he'd said to Edith. But what was he supposed to have done under the circumstances? They couldn't just stop this now, could they?

The smell of charred meat blended with the aromas of herbs and spices in the balmy air as Ana's father, along with Javi, prepared the cuts of beef for their dinner. His nose twitched at the paprika, oregano, garlic and parsley as it released its aromas on the open flame, the fat sizzling, popping and shooting even more tantalising odours into the night.

Usually he would have been up and dancing with his mother or Ana's mother by now. But now he could only sit and watch Ana doing her best to avoid him in her own parents' courtyard—talk about awkward. He'd probably scared her off, he thought in dismay, coming on too strong, getting over-excited about where this was going. Idiot! Trust him to get completely carried away with a romance when he should be focusing on his son.

Ines had been pretty relaxed about him having Javi tonight, but he was still in her bad books for… He couldn't remember what for now; there always seemed to be something. Oh yes, apparently the other day Javi had gone home asking Ines if he could have a Ouija board to contact the dead spirits in the cemetery. He supposed that was kind of *his* fault. Javi had overheard Ana and him laughing about how they'd tried it once, never mind that they'd failed to pick up any messages at all. And, now that he finally had Javi on a rare week night, without Ines firing texts at him every second, he was still getting distracted by a woman!

Eyeing Ana from across the courtyard, Gabriel sobered as he pondered their situation. Perhaps he'd pushed too hard, too fast with her. He should probably back off. Standing up, he crossed to the grill and spent the rest of the night helping Ana's father show Javi how to man an asado while, as if reading his mind, Ana disappeared to the kitchen with their mothers to help prepare salads, roasted vegetables and sauces.

Gabriel took a break to chase fireflies with Javi. The little bugs always came out at dusk, and Javi was obsessed with them. Every now and then, he'd catch Ana watching them through the window, their eyes would meet and his head would reel all over again.

There was something between them that could not be ignored—something electric and undeniable every time they were in close proximity. From their open conversations about careers and obligations one minute, to passionate whispers about their dreams and desires lying next to each other in one of their beds the next—every moment they spent together felt as if it was charged with an energy all its own. But, right now, she wouldn't come outside until Javi literally ran over and urged her to come by holding her hands.

'Ana, Ana, come see what we caught.'

Her wheelchair got stuck on a patch of weeds for a few seconds on her way over. Gabriel saw her father put down the asado utensil he was holding and start to head towards his struggling daughter. The look on Ana's face was a warning, but her father hadn't noticed.

Quickly Gabriel held up a hand to stop him. 'Don't,' he mouthed, stopping him in his tracks. All the man saw was his beloved daughter in trouble, and as a father himself Gabriel understood that much, but the last thing Ana needed was everyone rushing to help her all the time. She noticed his little warning gesture, just as her chair came unstuck and her face softened somewhat as she mouthed, 'Thank you.'

The tension lifted a little, but he pretended nothing had happened as she studied the fireflies in the jar Javi was showing her.

'Your father and I used to do this as children,' Ana said to Javi, looking at Gabriel through the other side of the glass as she held it up in the glow of the fairy lights. 'There used to be more fireflies than this, though. Thousands of them.'

'I remember,' Gabriel said, picturing her as a girl in this very garden, running around with him, catching fireflies. If only he'd known to run with her even more while they could, or to warn her not to get in the damned car that day.

'Really? Thousands?' Javi was staring into the jar, mesmerised by the tiny glowing bugs. 'I can't imagine you being young, Papa. Or you, Ana.'

'Well, we were.' She smiled, sighing softly. Without thinking, Gabriel put a hand to hers and squeezed it tightly. Straight away, the adrenaline coursed up his arm and around his brain. What he really wanted to do was wrap her fully in his arms and run away with her.

Somewhere by the table he heard their mothers gasp and immediately start gossiping. He dropped Ana's hand, dragging his fingers over his hair. Stupid him, thinking they'd 'just been invited for dinner' again. Javi seemed oblivious to the under-currents, content to hang out with Ana and him wherever they were, but it was clear that their families were all keeping tabs on what was proving to be a pretty obvious relationship. At least, he thought now, glancing at Ana, it *had* been pretty obvious to him till today.

Ana was trying to relax under the stars and fairy lights with all this love surrounding her, but somehow she just felt torn. As Javi practised his bowling skills with a set her parents had bought, she struggled not to feel as if this unit was probably the nicest thing she'd been a part of for years. It was, it was amazing. But what if it cost her everything else she'd worked so hard for? Love was nothing but a distraction and love for Gabriel… Well, she'd already learned the hard way years ago how much *that* could hurt.

It wasn't Gabriel's fault he wore his heart on his sleeve—in fact, that was one of the things she loved most about him. Of course he hadn't meant to make things weird by telling Edith they were 'in love'. She'd been angry at herself more than him today, for putting her own career and reputation in jeopardy. His confession, whether it had been just for Edith's sake or not, *had* felt pretty wonderful to hear…

'Ana, Ana, it's your turn,' Javi called now, urging her to the makeshift bowling ground and handing her a ball.

'Do your best, Ana,' Gabriel quipped, and when she caught his eye a spark sent her heart beating harder in a flash. Why could she not just turn this thing off between them—this thing that now seemed to claim her mind, body and soul whenever he so much as said her name? She had no doubt it was mutual; she could practically feel the heat of his every glance brush against her skin, making her heart race even faster. Yet here they were, both trying to maintain some kind of

distance for everyone else's sake. Well, mostly
for her sake, she realised now.

Just today, they'd been caught, properly caught
making out like teenagers, and all of it had been
entirely unprofessional. What was she doing,
risking everything she'd worked for? If this all
blew up in her face, she'd have nothing left. People talked around here—not that they didn't talk
about her enough already, being the only doctor
in the barrio confined to a wheelchair with her
very own practice.

With a deep breath, Ana took aim and threw
the ball with all her might. It was a strike, to her
surprise. The whole group cheered behind her
and she grinned back at them, feeling a little bit
victorious, especially in front of her parents. Taking another look at Gabriel, she didn't miss his
proud smile. *Curses!* She had been all ready to
take a step back from it all, but here Gabriel was,
doing everything right. He had even somehow
stood up to Ines and managed to get Javi here this
evening when it was supposed to have been her
time with their son, something he'd never been
able to do till now. Ines always seemed to have
plans for Javi on their nights at home together.
But here they all were, and it felt so good.

'What do you think, Ana?' Javi stopped in
front of her, hands on his hips, lips pouting.

'Sorry, what was that, honey?' She'd zoned

out again, lost in her own thoughts. Gabriel eyed her uncertainly as he rearranged the balls on the lawn.

'I said, maybe I can sleep at your place tonight? Papa says I can't stay at his.'

Ana frowned. 'Why can't you stay at your papa's?' she said, more in Gabriel's direction.

'Your mother wants you at home tonight, you know that,' he said sternly and, as if on cue, he pulled out his phone, no doubt to check for her messages. Ana sighed and refrained from an eyeroll, which wouldn't have been entirely fair. Of course Ines wanted her son at home, just as Gabriel wanted him at *his* home, but Ines always got her way. She supposed it was too good to be true that they might be allowed to have him for more than a few hours on one of 'her' nights.

'Well, if your mama wants you home, I can't very well let you stay at my place, can I?' she reasoned gently with the boy. Javi looked upset. His lip quivered for a second as he stared at the ground and she saw the same raging emotions in him that she often saw in Gabriel, before he managed to curb them one way or another. It would have been cute if it wasn't slightly concerning. Gabriel was still at Ines's beck and call, after all, worried about putting so much as a toe wrong in case she went for full custody. But what about what Javi wanted?

'I don't want to go home,' he said now, balling his little fists.

Gabriel was at his side in a second, crouching on the grass. 'Why not, *mijo*?'

'I just don't.'

Ana was well aware of her father's and Gabriel's eyes on her, but she had to focus on Javi. She didn't want him feeling bad, not tonight when they'd all had such a lovely time together. How could she make this right?

'Javi, I can't let you stay tonight, but how about this? I'm free the night before your pawrents' day, so why don't you both come over with Savio for a sleepover? We'll order a takeaway and watch movies all night long and eat popcorn till we're stuffed.'

She smiled at him in encouragement and the little boy's face lit up as he nodded eagerly, all tears forgotten. 'I'm sure your mama won't mind that,' she added, glancing at Gabriel. He was looking at her slightly in awe now, as if he was both perplexed and grateful that she could wipe his son's bad mood away so easily. Javi's face was still shining with excitement as he took his turn at bowling. While she knew she'd got herself into something else with Gabriel when she'd just been questioning whether it was right to even keep this thing going—whatever it was—it wasn't fair to let Javi down.

She was starting to love him being around, actually. Already she could picture him in the cute giraffe onesie she'd seen in the kids' shop around the corner. Maybe she shouldn't get so excited just yet, she thought when, as predicted, Gabriel started saying his goodbyes and bundling Javi up, ready to take him home. It wasn't even eight o'clock.

Ana feigned a smile, but she could feel her shoulders tense, watching the way the boy slowed his steps again, taking longer than necessary in the bathroom while Gabriel stood outside, urging him to hurry up. Javi didn't want to leave, and she didn't want him to go either. A sudden tightness in her chest told her that, no matter what either of them did or said, she was caught up in a situation that was increasingly out of her control.

'Ines wants him...' he started to say to her on the driveway after Javi had reluctantly hugged everyone goodbye, but she didn't let him finish.

'I know,' she said quietly. 'It can't be helped. Go, get him home.'

He shot her an apologetic look over his shoulder before they finally left.

Later, alone in her bed, she couldn't fight the inner turmoil from raging as it kept her from another night of decent sleep. She was getting all caught up in this when she had important work to focus on, when Gabriel had his son, his work commitments and Ines to placate around the clock. Wasn't this all getting far too complicated?

It was hard to imagine actually calling things off, though. Maybe she just needed a little more time, she reasoned with herself and the bedroom ceiling. Maybe she was starting to need Gabriel and Javi in her life more than she'd realised, which was why all this was affecting her more than any relationship ever had before. And that, right there, was the problem.

Since when had she *needed* anyone except herself? Well, OK, since always…but it wasn't something she particularly enjoyed admitting; in fact, it sat well outside of her comfort zone. What if Gabriel went all in with her and then something else happened, besides Ines, to make him decide it was all too much?

She simply had to call things off before she… before *anyone*…got badly hurt, including Javi, who seemed quite besotted with her already. It simply had to be done now while they could still go back to being friends.

CHAPTER FOURTEEN

THE PARK WAS flooded with sunshine as Ana stopped her chair beside Gabriel and Javi. She was a little late getting to the pawrents' day event from the clinic, after Ebony had arrived late herself, but it was even more nerve-racking waiting for Javi's turn to demonstrate the tricks he'd been teaching Savio. The kid didn't look fazed, though. His grin spread from ear to ear as he waved at her excitedly around Gabriel, stroking Savio's soft head next to him, watching the other dogs and his school friends on the agility trail.

Ana felt a flush of pride, watching the sun catch in the kid's cute black curls, and then another flurry of nerves as Gabriel pressed his hand over hers, a sign that he was glad to see her.

'He's up next,' he said.

'Mmm.' She kept her eyes on the canine activities, wishing she wasn't such a coward. It was just that she liked him too much for her own good. Even his hand on hers in public made her want to grab him by the collar and pull him astride her, like she had last night in her living room before he'd carried her up to bed. How could she listen to her head about breaking things off when her heart was still pounding for him around the clock?

Infuriatingly, she hadn't yet managed to have that important discussion with him; she hadn't even come close! In fact, Gabriel's overnight bag was still in the car, after the fun night they'd all had last night at her place. They had stayed up late watching old black-and-white films and eating popcorn as promised, with Javi in between Gabriel and her on the sofa, and Savio sprawled lazily on the floor. She'd felt so happy, content and at peace with life, sitting there with candles flickering on the coffee table, listening to their laughter and joining in with their happy father-son banter. Javi had looked so cute in the giraffe onesie, too. She hadn't been able to resist picking it up for him.

After they'd put him to bed in the spare room, she and Gabriel had made love till the early hours. They were getting good at it. Too good: it was highly addictive. She had hoped that she'd be able to suggest an amiable departure from this new-found couple status of theirs, but this need to call it off, while justified, was starting to feel a lot like self-sabotage.

Over the last few days, whenever she'd made

her mind up to put an end to what would surely only go wrong sooner or later, Gabriel had done something so right it had turned her stomach into a flock of butterflies. Maybe she'd let her own stupid fears of rejection get in the way of going all in, she decided now as Javi was finally called into the arena with Savio. And who could blame her? Not all men had it in them to handle her independence and her ambitious, unstoppable nature, let alone her disability, but somehow all that seemed easy-breezy to Gabriel.

And now, here they were at the pawrents' day. She was actively abandoning her duties at the clinic to be with them both again: did that make her a stand-in parent of sorts? It was everything she'd always said she would never do—put a man between herself and all she'd worked for, and a child too for that matter—but secretly she was absolutely loving it. So what was she supposed to do?

Pretty soon, Javi and Savio were performing the tricks they'd practised nightly like a well-oiled machine. As soon as the whistle blew, they dove straight into their routine. She watched in awe, listening to Gabriel's proud fatherly words of encouragement as Savio responded to each of Javi's commands with speed and accuracy. The dog leaped gracefully through an obstacle course of hoops and tunnels, then stood up on his hind legs while Javi commanded him to salute, do a barrel roll and then a paw-shake, much to the roar of the adoring crowd.

'Woo!' Gabriel let out the hugest cheer when Savio's fluffy paw touched Javi's hand, and Ana couldn't help going one better by wolf whistling. Several people turned to look, including Gabriel, and she shrugged.

'Something you have to learn when you can't move very fast,' she told him. 'Sometimes I need attention.'

'Like the attention you demanded from me last night?' he whispered seductively into her ear, and her whole ear turned red and tingled. He left a hand resting on her shoulder and she sighed in contentment. She had definitely been over-thinking this whole thing—why could she not just be happy to be in this new, wonderful situation?

With each trick that Javi and Savio performed, the audience clapped and cheered even louder. Savio started to spin round in circles, and Javi kept up with every twist and turn, till they were doing their own orchestrated dance. Ana's eyes widened as she watched this display of teamwork between boy and dog; it was almost too cute for words! Then, before she knew it, she was being called to demonstrate the trick they'd all mastered together.

'I believe in you,' Gabriel said now, feigning total seriousness before dropping a kiss to her lips. Suddenly a little nervous, she almost latched onto him like a monkey, but Javi was looking on and clapping in encouragement, so she broke away and made her way into the circle. Soon, Savio was running across the grass from Javi straight onto her lap in the wheelchair, and Javi was pretending to control her chair to reel them both back towards him on an invisible rope.

When they'd finished their routine, the audience erupted in more applause, and she bowed from her seated position, half-embarrassed at all the attention, but proud of Javi. Ana could see the tenderness in Gabriel's gaze when it wandered from Javi to her especially when, moments later, the judges announced he and Savio the winners and placed a huge, shiny gold medal around his neck in the shape of a paw.

'Amazing!' Gabriel enthused at them both, high-fiving Javi, then her. She was just about to suggest he join them for the team photo with the other parents, the kids and their dogs when she realised his phone was buzzing with the sound reserved for Ines. Watching him reach for his pocket at lightning speed, her heart sank on the spot, but this time she just couldn't hold her tongue…

* * *

Gabriel knew he'd messed up just from the look on her face. 'You don't have to always pander to her! She knows Javi is fine,' she said.

'I know that.' He frowned, retracting his hand, surprised at her acerbic tone. 'She just wants to…'

'To what? To remind you of something you already know, like the fact that she's collecting Javi in twenty-five minutes in the car park by the basketball court? We all know that.'

Gabriel bit his cheek and sighed through his nose. OK, so it annoyed Ana that he was constantly answering to Ines, but this was the first time she'd been snappy about it—not that he could blame her.

'I'm not answering,' he said as his phone continued to demand his attention. He could almost picture Ines scowling in annoyance at the other end of the line, probably in the car somewhere. She loved to call from the car. Ines would hold this against him as being a mark of disrespect. Maybe she'd use it later as evidence for her keeping Javi in her full custody.

'I'm not answering,' he told her again, and she nodded, even though she still seemed upset.

'Hey,' he said, reaching for her hand. 'I'm sorry.'

'I know you are,' she said, and her ensuing silence burned. They'd been having such a nice time, but of course this must have been getting on her nerves for a while. He always put Javi first, and with that priority came a whole lot of Ines. But Ana had to come equal first now. This new relationship was just as important to him. Ines did probably just want to remind him that she was due to pick up Javi soon, as if he didn't have the place and time drummed into his skull already. He was increasingly embarrassed at how he was always forced to talk to her and reconfirm all these arrangements in front of Ana.

'Your mama's going to come get you soon,' he told Javi, feeling Ana's eyes on him, as if she knew damn well he was itching to pick up the phone still buzzing angrily in his pocket.

'What? Already?' Javi didn't look pleased. He bunched his red T-shirt at the bottom in his fists and his eyes clouded over with a sudden frustration and helplessness that jarred Gabriel.

'You must be excited to show her your medal? She'll be so pleased you won,' Ana assured him. She pulled out a treat for Savio and petted his fuzzy head affectionately. 'She'll want to see Savio, too.'

'No, can't we stay with you again?' Javi pouted, playing with the medal around his neck.

'Not tonight, but soon,' she said kindly, and Gabriel felt the dismay behind her words as she looked at him. Damn; his phone was ringing *again*.

'Yes, we'll do that again soon,' he confirmed.

'When? Why can't I stay tonight? I don't want to go home!'

Gabriel looked at his son in despair. Javi had been saying this quite frequently lately, but had never said why. On one hand, it was nice, knowing Javi wanted to spend more time with him, but what the heck was going on with Ines? He would have to talk to her, but not today. Ana came first, before his issues with Ines, he decided. He was going to take her out to dinner tonight and ask her to be his girlfriend officially. The thought filled him with nerves, but *that* was what he had to focus on now. He thought about the cosy, candlelit restaurant he had chosen and how romantic it would be—as long as she said yes.

Flustered, he said, 'Javi, how about we go for an ice-cream before we leave? Come on, I bet they have chocolate mint. Ana, do you want one?'

'I'll stay here with Savio,' she said, and on hearing his name the dog leapt for her cheek with a big lick. She laughed and Gabriel instantly felt better. 'We don't want to tempt him with ice-cream, he might knock the stall over. He's not *that* well trained yet, are you, boy?'

He left her talking to some of the other parents and ordered their ice-cream at the stand, try-

ing to imagine what might happen this evening
at the restaurant. Maybe he would wait till after
the starter, so he could ask her before the mains
arrived. Then they could toast each other with
champagne.

Glancing back at her, he watched her laughing
with a woman in a blue dress, patting Savio as
though the dog had always been hers. She loved
that dog as much as Javi did, he thought, unable
to stop the silly grin from taking over his face as
the guy behind the ice-cream stall handed him
his cones.

'Mint choc-chip for you, sir,' Gabriel said,
swinging round to Javi. But Javi wasn't there.
What? He'd been standing right next to him
just seconds before and now...where the heck
was he? He couldn't have simply disappeared.
Anxiety seized Gabriel's heart as he frantically
scanned the crowd for his son. Stumbling forward, he promptly handed both ice-creams to a
bewildered young boy and headed for Ana, fear
taking over his confusion as he imagined all the
'what if?'s. His mind spinning a million miles a
second, he couldn't help imagining the reaction
Ines would have if anything happened to Javi
on *his* watch.

Ana seemed to sense something had happened
and rushed up to him in her chair, her eyes wide
with concern. 'What's wrong? Where is he?'

Gabriel tried to keep it together. 'He's gone—
I don't see him. Did you see him?'

'No, he was with you. Try not to panic, Gabriel,
he can't have gone far. Savio, can you help find
Javi?' she said to the dog, who was still trailing
them, wagging his tail as if they were embark-
ing on some grand, exciting adventure. Unfortu-
nately, though, Savio hadn't been trained to locate
missing people any more than he'd been trained
not to beg for ice-cream.

'Oh God, Javi...' Gabriel groaned, gripping
his hair, every muscle tense beneath his shirt.
All around them people were enjoying themselves, kids running here and there, but he felt
as if his heart was going to burst out of his chest
with panic. All he could feel was the coldness of
mounting dread as he and Ana searched every
corner of the park for Javi's small figure, calling
out his name.

'Where did he go, Ana?'

'I don't know.' He felt a chill run down his
spine as she said it but just the look on her face
kept him together. She was concerned, but still
dead calm. Despite what was happening, she carried herself with a confidence that he drew from
as he sucked in breath after breath after breath.
People came to him with emergencies every day
and he couldn't deal with theirs fast enough...
but this was Javi.

The minutes passed like hours, until finally Ana grabbed his arm. 'Let's split up. You go that way, I'll go this way with Savio. Keep your phone close.

'Come, Savio boy, let's find Javi!'

CHAPTER FIFTEEN

ANA'S HEAD WAS spinning faster than her wheels as she found herself scanning the periphery of the park, looking for Javi. 'Where are you?' Through clenched teeth she found herself murmuring prayers that hadn't left her mouth in years. Javi had only been gone a matter of minutes but she'd never seen Gabriel so distressed and it tore at her heart to see him that way. Javi was his whole world. Her heart had started beating a strange kind of warning back there, when he'd clutched at his hair as if he wanted to break something or… well…run away. There had never been a maternal bone in her body, but she knew this little boy very well by now. There was something important that he wasn't telling them.

A motion from the play park caught her eye, and Savio was alert now too. His ears pricked up, then he darted like a lightning bolt ahead of her towards the swings. At first she saw only the empty swings swaying on their chains in the breeze but, as she pulled closer, a flash of red alerted her to the bushes behind the climbing tower. *Javi?*

Savio got to him first, and Javi tried to push the dog off as he nuzzled his shoulder and cheeks. Javi was crouched down in a bush, his tiny body trembling as he hugged his knees. He was clutching his left arm to his body protectively.

Instincts primed, Ana leaned over him. 'Oh, honey, what happened?' She could see that he was trying to muffle his sobs, but still they escaped from him in short, painful bursts as he winced.

'My arm!'

'What's wrong with your arm, *mijo*?' Reaching for her phone, she called Gabriel.

'I fell from the tower!' Javi wailed.

Ana stroked Javi's hair soothingly, murmuring words of reassurance as she helped him up. Already she could see Gabriel sprinting towards them from the other side of the park.

'We're getting you some help. Why did you run away, honey? Why did you try and hide in the tower?'

'I don't want Mama to take me away!' he cried, just as Gabriel reached them and swept the little boy up into his arms. Ana's heart hammered as she explained what had happened. Savio did his best to lick Javi's tears away as Gabriel put his son down again, tearing at his own shirt to make a makeshift sling for the boy. Why didn't Javi want Ines to collect him?

Gabriel, now a picture of sculpted perfection in just his faded jeans, stood with his back turned to her. His tanned flesh rippled with each movement as he held his phone to his ear and spoke to Bruno, his muscles flexing beneath the skin. The lines on his face were etched deep when he turned back to her.

'Bruno's coming with the ambulance,' he said, before crouching down on his haunches, all his attention on Javi, who was still whimpering in pain. He called Ines next. It wasn't good, Ana could tell: the woman's voice was audible down the line, even as Ana sat three feet away with Javi, still holding his arm in the shirt sling. Ines sounded furious with Gabriel, as if this was his fault!

'It's not your fault, you know,' she tried to tell him, but he didn't seem to hear her.

All Ana could do was stay there, watching the distress cloud Gabriel's eyes. In this moment she wanted nothing more than to take away his emotional pain, but the anguished expression on his face broke her heart, and she realised she'd never felt this helpless. Of course he would blame himself.

Eventually the ambulance rumbled onto the road beyond the hedges, and in seconds Bruno and one of his young trainees were hurrying into the play park with a first-aid kit and a stretcher, while a crowd gathered around behind the fence. The young paramedic checked Javi's vital signs before examining the arm with ultimate diligence. She tapped and prodded gently, conferring with Bruno and Gabriel, and Ana watched the creases around Gabriel's eyes deepening again when Javi winced in pain. They all knew it was broken.

'It's definitely broken,' Bruno confirmed, ruffling Javi's hair gently. 'You're very brave, bud; I know it hurts. Let's get you to the hospital.'

'I'll come too,' Ana said before she could think, but Gabriel looked at her, then Savio.

Oh, right.

'You're right—we can't bring the dog,' she said as Savio licked at Javi's fingers while they helped him onto the stretcher. The distress mounted inside her as she felt increasingly redundant, but she sprang into action as best she knew how, summoning the dog. 'I'll take him home, then catch you up,' she told them, trying to keep her eyes as well as her hands from his exposed chest. More than anything she itched to pull him closer, or offer some kind of extra reassurance, which she was becoming increasingly aware that she could not provide. He didn't want her support. Gabriel merely nodded at her and quickly followed the others towards the ambulance.

* * *

A&E was as busy as ever, and Gabriel sat stiffly in the shirt Bruno had lent him. His friend Sofia, the trauma surgeon, had found him. Being as fond of Javi as she was, she'd been worried and had rushed to check on him. 'What's going on with our little *mijo*?' she asked now. 'And you? You look... Oh, Gabe.'

Gabriel accepted her comforting hug, realising he'd missed her since he'd been combining his shifts with the ambulance staff and the clinic. Not that she needed his friendly ear as much, now that she and Carlos Cabrera were an item.

'Things are OK,' he said. Javi's arm was now in a cast and, instead of crying, he'd seemed quite intrigued by the hospital once the painkillers were doing their job. He kept asking what this instrument was for, and what that machine did. 'How are you and Carlos doing?' he asked her, unable to stop a little sly nudge and wink.

Sofia bit back a smile, looked around her and leaned in conspiratorially. 'We are doing better than great,' she said, her pretty mouth breaking out into a fully fledged grin. He was about to ask for more juicy gossip when Ines swung through the door like a hurricane.

'I came as soon as I could, but the traffic was terrible... Oh, Javi!'

She rushed straight through to her son, speaking rapidly, checking his arm and then looking for any other injuries, dropping a flurry of kisses to his face and head. Then she stepped back and locked eyes with Gabriel. Sofia made her swift departure with a squeeze of his hand and he stood, bracing himself. Ines was a formidable woman—as tall as him, and statuesque, with the kind of beauty that drew attention wherever she went. Today being no exception as she glowered at him from beneath her heavy black fringe, causing the nursing assistant to excuse herself from the room.

'You were supposed to be watching him,' she admonished. Her dark eyes glinted with anger and indignation as she crossed her arms over her chest. 'What if something worse had happened?'

'I'm OK, Mama,' Javi insisted groggily, wiping lipstick from his cheeks. He was still wearing his medal, which glinted in the harsh lights above. Ines tapped her nails on her arms and shifted in the silk trousers that accentuated her curves. It was clear where Javi had inherited his fiery temperament from; Ines wanted answers and she wanted them now.

He was about to ask her why Javi hadn't wanted to go home to her in the first place when the door opened and Ana appeared. His heart leapt to his throat.

'Sorry to interrupt,' she started, before Javi called out to her.

'Ana! Look at my cool cast. Bruno and the nurse said I can get people to sign it later.'

'Very cool,' she said, though she was frowning in Ines' direction now. He watched the two women size each other up. Suddenly he was more aware than ever of how different they were. Of course, they had met before, on that beach trip to Pinamar when Ines had been pregnant while they'd been trying to make things work. It only just struck him now how Ana had always made some kind of excuse as to why she couldn't stick around with them for long.

'Good to see you again,' Ana said politely. 'It's been a long time.'

'Hmm,' was Ines' cool reply. She stared at Ana, who was still holding a wrapped gift she had bought for Javi. 'I see now why Gabriel has been so distracted.'

Ana bit her lip and turned away and a surge of rage thundered through Gabriel that he had to suppress. He stood between them, lowering his voice so Javi couldn't hear. 'Ines, that's enough. Ana has nothing to do with this. What's going on with you?'

Ines blew air through her nostrils and looked between them. Her voice hardened as she glared at them. 'I just worry about Javi, that's all.'

'I know you do, but he's fine,' Gabriel told her, shooting a sideways look at Ana. He felt so bad at the way Ines was acting, and for dragging Ana into this mess. Hearing that Javi was fine wasn't enough for Ines, clearly. No sooner had the nurse arrived to discharge him, than Ines was whisking him away, insisting on carrying all his things to her parked car. Gabriel followed with Ana close behind, telling Javi he would see him later as Ines helped him carefully into the car. Once the door was shut, she turned to him, glaring again.

'This should not have happened—you're his father.'

'What's that supposed to mean?'

Ines just glowered at him a second longer before stalking to the other side of the car. In less than thirty seconds he was watching her pull out of the hospital car park. Ramming his hands in his hair, it was another moment before he remembered Ana was behind him. She was watching him closely, Javi's gift still on her lap.

'That went well,' he said drily. He crossed to her. 'Ana, I'm so sorry you had to witness all that.'

'It's not all your fault,' she replied as he took her hand.

'But she was right—I'm his father. I wasn't paying close enough attention to him.'

Ana sighed deeply, and to his shock she gen-

tly pulled her hand away from him. In the back-
ground he caught Bruno loading some supplies
into the ambulance, watching them carefully, pretending he wasn't. 'I'm sorry, Gabriel.'

The look on her face sent his pulse to his throat.
Sorry? 'Why are you sorry?'

She shook her head, her expression flashing
with pain for just a second. 'Ana?'

'I have to go,' she said, her voice strained now.
'Can't we talk?'

'What about, Gabriel? This isn't going to work.
There's just too much going on with you and Ines,
and Javi, and you don't need me complicating
things further.'

Dread coiled in his stomach at her words. 'How
are you complicating things?'

She inhaled sharply. Sadness and regret flared
around her irises as their eyes locked. 'I haven't
been paying attention either, Gabriel, and we've
both been distracted and preoccupied lately.
We've both forgotten what really matters. I think
we should just go back to being friends, don't
you? I know you have a shift at the clinic tomorrow, but I'll ask Ebony to come in.'

The words felt like a punch to his chest, not
what he wanted to hear at all. He stood taller,
feeling his composure start to wane the more he
searched her eyes for a hint that she didn't mean
it. But she was clearly deadly serious. How long

had she been feeling this way? Suddenly he could tell she'd been having these reservations for a while—he'd just been too stubborn to admit it to himself. Ana didn't need all this drama in her busy life, and this was her polite way of excusing herself from a difficult situation before she became even more tangled up in it all.

'I don't think I can go back to just being your friend,' he admitted with a frown. It was the truth. 'But don't bother Ebony. I won't let the clinic down.'

'I'm sorry,' she said again. Before he could so much as take her hand, or tell her how much he regretted dragging her so deeply into this mess, she turned away from him and sped her chair towards the exit faster than he'd ever be able to keep up.

CHAPTER SIXTEEN

ANA HAD ALWAYS prided herself on her ability to stay focused in the face of chaos. But there was something about the way Gabriel's eyes met hers across the brightly lit examination room that threatened to shatter her composure. The tension that had been simmering between them all morning was still there, humming beneath the surface, and now it crackled in the air as they prepared to discuss expat Evelyn Sinclair's case.

'Mrs Sinclair, thank you for coming in today,' Gabriel began, placing the medical chart down on the bed, his voice steady and reassuring. It was the opposite to how he'd been yesterday, when he'd been wracked with despair over the missing Javi, and then consumed with guilt and dread in the face of his ex's fury.

'Can you tell us about your symptoms—when they started and how they've progressed?'

The room was filled with the soft hum of medical equipment and the faint scent of antiseptic mingled with Gabriel's fresh, familiar scent as

Evelyn started recounting her fatigue and her achy limbs. Ana made notes, but her mind kept drifting as she tried not to look at Gabriel. He'd been so cool with her since she'd called things off. He hadn't even tried to talk to her about it, almost as if he knew they'd be better off as friends. Maybe he'd change his mind about not wanting to be friends, she thought hopefully, though it didn't feel right to her either any more. How on earth could they put something so wonderful into reverse so quickly?

They would just have to try.

She had slept with his scent surrounding her in bed last night despite the absence of him. Clutching the pillow he'd last slept on, she had let the tears fall, agonising over what she'd done. She had to let him go, though. She was doing the right thing, wasn't she? Surely he realised she was simply getting in the way? Javi was everything to him, and now, after the incident in the park, Gabriel was probably even more terrified that Ines was going to go for full custody. He had always been Ana's rock, had always been there to support her, even when she'd insisted he and everyone else leave her alone. It was only fair that she release him now and let him focus fully on his son.

Evelyn's voice wavered as she continued, looking at Gabriel. 'It started about six months ago.

First the tiredness, no matter how much rest I got. My muscles felt so weak, and my skin…it became so sensitive that even the slightest touch was painful. My hair started falling out and my nails turned brittle. I've lost weight, despite eating more than usual, and I have trouble sleeping.'

'That's quite the list,' Ana said, catching Gabriel's eye.

'Not being able to sleep is the worst,' Gabriel said directly to Ana. OK, so that was a dig. She had clearly kept him from sleeping, as much as her abrupt decision to end things had kept her from nodding off until well after three a.m.

'The last clinic I went to didn't know what was wrong with me,' Evelyn continued. 'Lately, I've been having trouble swallowing, and my voice is hoarser than it should be. Can you hear it?'

Ana nodded. 'Have you experienced any mood changes or emotional symptoms?' she asked.

Evelyn hesitated, her eyes dropping to her lap. 'Yes, I've been feeling depressed and anxious. It's been hard to concentrate and remember things. I just haven't felt like myself lately.'

'I know what you mean,' Ana muttered under her breath as she made for the store cabinet, letting Gabriel explain that they would have to run some tests, including blood work and imaging. It was getting near on impossible to ignore the way her own emotions were fraying around him, but the clinic came first, as did her reputation. She was not about to let a brief love affair ruin anything for her, any more than she was willing to complicate things for Gabriel and Javi.

Ana was still fighting her own wavering emotions by the time they were alone again. It was just herself and Gabriel, analysing tests, discussing symptoms and reviewing Evelyn's case, while the big fat elephant still stood unaddressed in the middle of the room.

Gabriel sat on the examination table, staring at her over the edge of a medical chart. Her pulse quickened when their eyes met but she kept her voice calm. 'It appears that Evelyn has an auto-immune disorder that's attacking her thyroid,' she said. 'We'll put together the treatment plan, starting with...'

'This is so weird,' Gabriel said suddenly, slamming the file on the bed and gripping the edge of it. His dark eyes bore into her as she felt the sweat prickle on the back of her neck 'Don't you think it's weird? I'm not sure, now I'm actually here, that I can work with you any more, Ana. This should be my last day.'

His words felt like a gut punch. She sucked in a breath as he jumped from the bed, slowly spinning her chair round to him. 'I thought we could at least try and be friends, Gabriel...'

'I told you, that's not going to work for me,' he said curtly, and for a moment, the tension between them felt too strong to be contained. She thought he was about to grab her face, kiss her doubts away and remind her that they could and *should* never be platonic again, but his emotions stayed behind his eyes before he strode to the window and heaved a sigh at the glass.

'Well, Ebony's told me she can probably start coming in full-time,' she offered matter-of-factly, afraid that she was about to follow him and demand he kiss her, and that she'd been wrong to call things off.

Don't be weak, Ana, this is what you wanted! Didn't he see how this was best for him and for them? Somehow, though, the words wouldn't leave her mouth.

'Right, then,' he said, unbuttoning his coat while she felt the panic rise in her throat. 'If Ebony's free, that would be best.'

Ugh. He was being so cool now, it was sending an icy blast through her bloodstream, chilling her to the bone. She'd come to want him here at the clinic, she realised, overcome by her own selfishness suddenly as he stared out of the window with his back turned. To think she'd always thought she was the strong one, the independent warrior ploughing onwards, over anyone in her path. Now, the thought of him not being here any more, not being anywhere in her day-to-day existence, was really sinking in.

Later, at home, Ana sat in silence, prodding at a plate of pasta spirals. Her appetite was non-existent; all she kept thinking was how she would ever be able to go about her working day at the clinic without Gabriel, and without knowing she'd see Javi at the end of it.

What was wrong with Javi, anyway? It seemed as though he was increasingly frustrated about having to be at home with his mum and step-dad. The way Ines was reacting to the smallest things... OK, some of the bigger things too—the broken arm wasn't exactly a mother's dream, but it all spoke volumes about the other woman's unhappiness.

Her doctor's instincts were on alert. It was very clear when someone was stressed, and Ines was definitely highly stressed. Her mood swings were giving poor Gabriel whiplash. But it wasn't Ana's place to do anything about it.

The next day, Ana was eating lunch alone in the clinic's small staff room, watching the rain falling outside. Naturally she was thinking about Gabriel and Ines. She could hardly believe it when a cough behind her drew her attention back to the door, and there was the woman herself. Spinning round, she almost dropped her salad into her lap. 'Ines?'

'Your receptionist let me back here—I hope that's OK. I think we need to talk.'

'Yes…'

Ana studied Ines as she stepped fully inside, glancing warily at Ana from head to toe as Ana touched a hand to her flowery headband. Ines was the opposite of her when it came to style. She wore a crisp white blouse tucked into dark-washed high-waisted jeans and wore cream-coloured ankle boots. Her hair was loose, framing her face in long waves that reached down to her collarbone. She was stunning but there was an air of sadness about her.

'I'm sorry for how I reacted yesterday,' Ines said, taking a plastic seat at the small table. 'I know you've grown quite close with Javi, and he's very fond of you too. I just thought, maybe I owed you an explanation. Things have been a little off lately.'

Ana nodded, debating with herself whether it was right to do this or not. Would Gabriel think this was gossiping, or her sticking her nose in where it wasn't wanted? What was the point of getting involved when she had already excused herself from their lives anyway? Hadn't she decided just last night that it wasn't her place to get involved in this…whatever it was? But, then again, whatever was up with Ines affected Gabriel and Javi too and, the more she thought about it, the more guilty she felt at doing nothing but walking away—so to speak. She'd done nothing to help Gabriel, when he'd *always* gone out of his way to be there for her.

'Javi's in reception—he wanted to see your children's toys,' Ines said. 'They're looking after him for me. Your staff are lovely, by the way.'

'They're the best.' Ana offered to make Ines some tea and she accepted.

'How is Pedro?' Ana asked, filling the kettle from the tap, hoping it didn't sound too much as though she was probing.

'He's working, as usual, locked away in his study,' came her cool reply, followed by a deep, resounding sigh.

Ana nodded. OK, then, so that was a pretty big hint as to why Ines might be unhappy. Something was going on with Pedro and her.

'It's mint,' Ana said a couple of minutes later, putting a cup of steaming tea down in front of her visitor and positioning her wheelchair at the opposite end of the table. Ines thanked her and sipped the sweet tea, and Ana wondered if it was acceptable to ask about the state of her marriage.

Ines sighed again, no doubt seeing the question in Ana's eyes and probably realising that there was no point in denying it. She put down her cup with a slightly trembling hand and looked away for a few seconds before finally speaking.

'We've been arguing a lot recently,' Ines admitted reluctantly. Her face dropped and she seemed to become smaller in her chair, as if someone had let out all of the air inside of her. Ana felt a pang of empathy for the woman.

'I'm sorry to hear that.'

'Javi has picked up on it, though we've tried not to argue in front of him. I feel so guilty...'

'Oh, Ines,' Ana said, suddenly torn. Tears began to well up in Ines' eyes as she started going into details about how busy Pedro was with his work, how they'd turned into strangers in the same house and how he never even bought her flowers any more. Ana felt overwhelmed. She reached out a hand across the table and clasped her fingers. Ines squeezed hers back. She hadn't expected Ines to open up so fast to her, but it seemed as if she'd been bottling this agony up inside for too long now, just waiting for someone to notice and listen.

'I suppose I can understand why Javi wants to stay with his papa, and you,' Ines conceded. 'I just feel so helpless, knowing I might lose him.'

Ana balked. Did Ines even know that Gabriel constantly worried that *he* might lose his son—

that Ines would ask for full custody? 'You won't lose Javi, Ines. You are his mother—he loves you.'

'Ana?' A small voice from behind the door made her start. Suddenly Javi appeared, his little hand in Maria's.

'Sorry, ladies, he was asking for you,' she said, releasing him into the staff room. Ana smiled at him as he walked to them in his cast, wearing a loose cotton shirt printed with robots and matching dark-blue trousers.

'What are you doing?' he asked them.

'I'm just talking with your mama.' Ana smiled. Ines promptly got up to refill their tea cups, and she felt Ines watching them as Ana asked how he was and finally handed over the gift she'd been keeping for him. Luckily, she'd had it stored there at the clinic in her locker. Ana's heart melted as he pulled out the stuffed toy—a dog that looked rather like Savio.

'I love it, thank you, Ana!' Javi hugged it tightly under his good arm as Ines put her refilled cup down and asked to see the toy.

For a second Ana thought a gift from her might have been a little unwelcome, but Ines shot her a look of gratitude over Javi's head as she swiped at her own tired eyes.

'Right, Javi, we didn't finish inspecting the fire engine out there,' Maria said, beckoning the boy back outside again with her. Ana knew she could tell they needed to talk. Ines dropped a kiss on his head. Javi kissed his mother's cheek and then, to Ana's surprise, turned to kiss hers too before heading back outside with Maria and his toy.

Ines watched him go. 'He likes you a lot,' she said.

Ana smiled. 'I like him a lot too.'

They both sat in silence for a moment and then Ines turned to her. 'I'm so sorry for how I've been acting lately,' she said, her voice barely above a whisper.

Ana shook her head. 'I think Gabriel feels like he's failing you,' she said, feeling empowered now and determined to make things right. 'But the truth is, Javi getting his arm broken in the park was just an accident. It wasn't Gabriel's fault, it wasn't anyone's fault.'

'I know.'

Ana reached out and squeezed Ines' hand once more. She could hardly imagine how difficult it must be to be a full-time parent, juggling a thousand things, always blaming yourself when things went wrong. Ana could understand now where Ines had been coming from—she'd never meant to blame Gabriel for anything, she'd just been frustrated at her own situation, feeling guilty and stressed.

Ines sat up straighter and composed herself. 'I appreciate you seeing me today, Ana, I do.'

'That's OK. And I know you'll talk to Gabriel soon and reassure him that this wasn't his fault.' Ana looked at her hopefully, hoping her message was coming across.

Ines nodded. 'I'll talk to Gabriel. I just didn't want him to think I wasn't doing my best as Javi's mother, you know?'

'You're doing your best as his parents—you both are,' she told her, relieved that Ines had come to see her and that now, hopefully, Ines would finally explain to Gabriel what had been going on.

'You're good for Gabriel, you know,' Ines said when Ana walked her to the door. 'You're together, aren't you, finally?'

Finally? Ana realised she must have be frowning in confusion. Ines smiled.

'I think I always knew Gabe and I wouldn't work out. I always thought he was in love with someone else.'

'You mean me?' Ana heard herself say, surprised at how it just came out of her so easily, and how the giant knot in her stomach reformed on the spot, tighter than ever.

Ines laughed. 'Yes, you!'

'Well, we're not together,' Ana told her, flustered suddenly.

Ines looked surprised. 'You're not? Why not?'

Ana drew her lips together and shook her head. 'We're just focusing on other things,' she said, although the second she said it she realised how hollow her words must sound to Ines, who'd come here because she had eyes and could tell something was going on between them. She was right, of course. The only thing Ana had been able to focus on for the last few weeks was Gabriel but, just as she did with everyone, she had pushed him away. Because of her, they were over.

Ines kissed her cheek and said she'd see her soon. Her insides were swirling with this new information. Ana couldn't help thinking that maybe, in another world, she and Ines might even have been friends.

CHAPTER SEVENTEEN

ANA WATCHED FROM across the room with a heavy heart as Carla helped one of the elderly patients out of her seat in the waiting room. Her returning assistant, now fully recovered from her Carnival injury, was a petite woman with short, dark, wavy hair and a warm smile who, like Ebony, had a calm presence that put many of the patients at ease right away. But neither of them was Gabriel. It felt wrong, not having Gabriel there beside her, helping out in his own unique way. It felt like for ever since she'd seen him, even though it had been less than a week, and she missed him more than she'd ever thought it was possible to miss anyone!

Her stomach tightened in a knot of longing and she struggled to contain her emotions. His cheerful personality had been like sunshine in the clinic, everyone had said so, and she couldn't help thinking that, without him, the place she had been dreaming about for so long lacked the one special something it needed most.

'Where's Gabriel?' she heard Evelyn ask Carla some time later. Evelyn directed the same question to her once she was seated in the consultation room. Of course, Gabriel had been here for her first visit, when they'd run the tests and discovered her thyroid was causing her complaints, so she wanted him to see to her this time too.

'He's not working here any more,' she said sadly, forcing a smile at the look Maria threw her as she put down a file, then closed the door. Maria knew how much Ana missed him; she had told her many times.

Carla was doing an amazing job, but they all knew it didn't compare with what Gabriel had brought to their team of healthcare providers. Every patient he had treated seemed to light up when they saw him walk into the room—even if they'd been feeling down or unwell when they'd first arrived. He had such a natural way of making everyone feel comfortable and reassured. And, as for her, she missed him at night. She missed the way he had made love to her. She'd probably never find that with anyone again, but he was clearly already over her. She'd not heard from him since he'd walked out.

The rain finally cleared later that day as Ana ran a small yellow duster over the leaves of her favourite fern. Everyone else had left for the day and it was just her here now, wrapping things up before they closed. She was taking her time. It was important to show her plants as much care as they showed the patients in this place, and she took pride each time she wiped the dust away from their delicate leaves.

But today, if she was really honest with herself, she just didn't want to go back home to her lonely, quiet apartment. Before starting this relationship with Gabriel, she hadn't felt lonely. It had just been normal for her, going home, reading her books, working, working some more, pretending to cook whilst heating up her mother's leftovers which she was still kindly leaving on Ana's doorstep, unasked for but much appreciated. Now, she spent most nights staring blankly at screens and pages, each one stretching ahead of her like an eternity.

She was just telling herself that there was no point in dwelling on what was over and done with, and that she'd be just fine with heating up another slice of lasagne and getting an early night, when a noise at the glass entrance door caught her ear. Wheeling herself round the corner, she stopped short in her chair.

'Savio?'

There was something on the little dog's collar. Moving forward and opening the door, she realised it was a beautiful, voluptuous orange marigold, just as the dog leapt for her lap, as if he couldn't wait to do his half of their well-practised trick. He sat there proudly, looking at her with his intelligent black eyes, and she stared back at him, not sure what to think.

'Did you escape, *mijo*?' she found herself asking the animal.

'He's with me,' came the voice. Peering over the dog's head, Ana's eyes widened as Javi stepped into view. He was also holding marigolds, a small bunch, which he held out to her as Savio leapt from her lap. She took them, breathing in their soft, subtle scent, too surprised to speak for a second.

'Javi, these are beautiful, but what are you doing here, and where's your…?'

The word 'papa' got stuck in her throat. Her question was answered before it even left her mouth. Stepping out from around the building, walking towards her, was Gabriel. She stared at him in disbelief. He was holding a bigger bunch of marigolds, so big it engulfed the top half of his body, before he moved them aside to reveal his handsome face.

'Gabriel.' Her hand flew to her mouth as he stopped in front of her. He was wearing a crisp white shirt, unbuttoned at the top to reveal his strong collarbone and gleaming dark skin. Oh, how she'd missed him. The deep-navy suit jacket paired with black trousers was complemented by the unruly mop of dark hair, as if he had been running his hands over it with nerves.

'Hi,' he said simply, holding out the flowers to her. 'These are for you.'

Taking them, her hand brushed his, shooting sparks right to her heart. As he fixed his penetrating gaze onto hers, she couldn't help but think that he was, without a shadow of a doubt, the most handsome man she had ever seen. But what was all this about?

He smiled at her, dimples peeking out on either side of his face, and all the days and nights she had spent apart from him melted away in an instant, even as the nerves settled back in. 'What is all this?'

He motioned for her to wheel her chair along next to him, and she let him help her lock the clinic doors. As they started down the street, with Javi talking to Savio just up ahead, she could feel her heartbeat in her throat.

'So, Ines got in touch…' he started, pressing his hands into his pockets. Ana clutched the flowers to her lap, wondering what had been said. She'd contemplated that maybe Gabriel would be angry with her for sticking her nose in, seeing as she hadn't heard from him till now.

'Thank you for talking to her,' he said, and

she sighed in relief. 'I know you were worried about Javi.'

'I just knew something was going on,' she admitted. 'I was worried about you too.'

'Well, I appreciate it. Ines has agreed to let me have Javi more often while she and Pedro work things out. I have you to thank for that.' He sighed and she realised he looked more anxious now than he had before when he'd showed up. 'I shouldn't have just quit on you, Ana, as a friend or co-worker...'

'Neither should I!'

'Working at the clinic with you, that's given me more than I ever knew I needed or wanted. Maybe some day, if you'll have me, I can work with you full-time?'

If you'll have me? Ana's mind was reeling now.

'It's not the same there without you,' she admitted, as the idea took seed in her mind and started sprouting in every direction. Of course she would take him on full time—everyone adored him.

'My *life* isn't the same without you,' he said. Gabriel stopped, glancing at Javi quickly. 'There's something I have to ask you.'

Ana sucked in a breath as he took her hand, turning it over in his, studying her fingers. Oh... he wasn't going to propose, was he? Suddenly her heart was a riot. This was something she had not been prepared for at all, not that she could imagine a future with anyone else. Of course, she would probably say yes if he asked, and maybe even move into his place if he didn't mind always carrying her to the bedroom...

'Will you be my best friend, now and always?' he said, cutting into her frenzied inner monologue.

What?

She stared at him, searching for words as the smile she knew and loved stretched out across his handsome face. Gosh she could look at those dimples for ever, but... 'Friend?'

'I want that, with you. But I also want you to be my girlfriend. Will you be both, Ana? I'm madly in love with you—you know that, don't you?'

Ana blinked, her mouth opening and closing several times before the words came tumbling out. 'Girlfriend? I mean...yes! Of course! I've wanted to be your girlfriend for so long, Gabriel.'

She felt her cheeks heat up with a blush as he smiled down at her, obviously pleased with her answer, even though she'd blurted it out at a million miles an hour. Luckily, there were no more words needed. Gabriel bent down to her slowly and closed the distance between them, his lips brushing hers ever so gently till she looped her arms around him and kissed him back even harder. Suddenly there was another brush of wetness on her cheek and she shrieked with laughter, pushing Savio away.

'Off, boy! This is not a kiss you can take over!'

Javi was giggling and clapping his hands in glee. 'Yay, Papa!' He ran up to greet them both with a huge hug that threatened to squish all her flowers, but she could hardly see a thing through the tears in her eyes.

She realised she was grinning like a teenager now as she looked from Javi to Gabriel. How could she not feel blessed, being here with two of the most important people in her life? And now she not only had her best friend back, she had an incredible, loving, kind, hotter-than-hot boyfriend too—not to mention his adorable son. Oh, and a dog, she thought, laughing again as Savio went in for another lick…

One year later

'Gabriel, come and try the cake!' Ana called out.

Gabriel disentangled himself from the increasingly knotted bunch of strings dangling around him. 'One second,' he called back from the top of the ladder. His house was already filled with decorations for Javi's birthday party but he needed to tie the last of the colourful balloons to the curtain poles. They were bobbing from every corner, as if they wanted to escape through the window and take flight in the sky, and it wouldn't do to release them before Javi and his friends had even seen them.

The smell of freshly baked cake had been wafting in from the kitchen all morning as Ana cooked, and the sweet vanilla essence already had him feeling hungry as he stepped into the kitchen. He couldn't help smiling at the sight of his beautiful girlfriend. Ana was covered in flour and her colourful patterned shirt was coated in a layer of fine dust as he leaned down to kiss her.

'My floury maiden,' he teased, and she laughed, handing him a small cupcake.

'Taste it! I made the main cake from the same mix.' She looked at him hopefully while he took a huge bite and chewed it, his eyes never leaving her face.

She wrinkled up her nose. 'Oh no, is it too sweet?'

'They're kids, they live on sugar,' he replied. 'It's perfect!'

Ana still looked nervous as she dabbed at her face and seemed only just to realise she was covered in flour. 'I should shower; Ines and Pedro will be here soon with Javi.'

'Want me to join you?' he asked, cocking an eyebrow, and before she could even answer he was swiping her giggling body up from her chair and making for the bathroom.

By the time they emerged from the bedroom,

hot and sweating after their shower, they were even later for the start of the party. Gabriel watched her dress in amusement. He didn't miss how she swiped up items of clothing from the drawers he'd cleared for her and put them back again straight away. When she decided on a floral printed dress with a green headscarf covered in peacocks, she promptly spilled the rest of her scarves and headbands from their box onto the floor.

'Hey, what's going on with you?' He laughed, racing to help gather them up. 'It's just a children's birthday party!'

Ana couldn't seem to look him in the eye. Something was wrong. He pressed a kiss to her lips, as if to calm her, and she sighed against his mouth. Then thankfully she smiled, but he could tell she was nervous about something.

'Everything's going to be great. The cake is delicious, the decorations are amazing and Javi will know how much effort you've put in,' he reassured her.

Ever since she'd moved into his place last year and they'd adapted the house for her wheelchair, she'd been going out of her way for Javi and him, and he was very much enjoying working more at the clinic. He did just three shifts a week with the ambulance team at the Hospital General de Buenos Aires, and the rest of the time he spent with her and the patients at the clinic was the perfect mix of action and calm for him at this stage in his life—but this was still Ana, of course. Everything had to be perfect. Most of the time now she let him help her, if only by calming her down. Hopefully she'd relax before Ines arrived...

Too late—the doorbell was ringing. They were here, and Javi's friends would be arriving in less than half an hour. Pressing another kiss to her lips, he said, 'You're perfect—I love you,' and hurried down the stairs.

Ana took a deep breath, staring at her reflection in the bedroom mirror. The peacocks on her headband seemed to be smirking at her. Why was she suddenly losing the ability to think straight? Gabriel—dear, sweet, wonderful, unsuspecting Gabriel—had no idea why she was so antsy. In fact, only Ines knew. Ines was her accomplice, her co-conspirator and...dared she say it?... friend.

She met Ines downstairs in the kitchen, where she was admiring the robot-shaped cake Ana had made, her arm looped through Pedro's. They both smiled warmly at her before Ines leant to kiss both her cheeks. Ana didn't miss the look in her eyes before she whispered, 'You've got this, Ana.'

Gabriel popped his head in. 'Are you guys coming? We're about to start "pass the parcel"!'

Gabriel had hung streamers from the windows to the doorway, and she felt as though she was floating as she entered the party with Ines and Pedro. Javi had invited ten of his closest friends over. Music filled the air and laughter echoed through the house as he ran around excitedly with his friends, dressed in an adorable sailor costume complete with captain's hat. He'd insisted on a fancy dress party. Even Savio had on a special costume—the poor dog was sitting a little grouchily on the floor in the corner, no doubt feeling sorry for himself, dressed as a giant watermelon.

Everyone else was enjoying themselves and, for a moment, she simply watched them all, drinking in their faces and listening to their conversations and laughter as the parcel went round and round the circle, stopping with the music to let another child tear off a layer, revealing a little gift inside.

It all felt like a dream, even though her nerves were now sky-high. Since Gabriel had asked her to move in a year ago, things had been pretty much perfect. As the most talked about couple in the district, not least because of their hugely successful practice, she was proud to be seen out and about at events and functions, and even prouder to be invited to couple's gatherings and family fun days with Gabriel and Javi. No more loneliness! She no longer felt the sting of sad nights by herself, and she'd even taken up cooking, much to her mother's delight.

Ana's mother had developed the special knack of arriving early at the weekend with a bundle of fresh ingredients and her recipe box. She would take over the kitchen, bustling to and fro as she chopped vegetables and simmered sauces, explaining every step as she worked.

Ana had felt awkward at first, but she had gradually come to understand that everything her mum did was out of deep love, respect and pride for her other more professional achievements. Accepting her parents' help every now and then didn't feel so suffocating, now that she had Gabriel to bring his light-hearted presence and sense of humour into every situation—she was happy to need him. She was even happier that he seemed to need her just as much in return.

The time had come. Ana steeled herself; there was no going back now. When the last layer of the parcel had been snatched up and torn into even smaller pieces by the watermelon dog, she wheeled herself to the front of the room, her heart beating a million miles a minute as she shifted slightly in her chair. Taking a couple of deep breaths, she reached into the pouch by her right thigh and called for Gabriel. She could see Ines was fighting a smile, while Pedro and Gabriel, who'd been chatting in the corner, just looked confused.

'Gabriel, you've made me think a lot this past

year,' she started, as he dropped to the couch just by her side and ran his hands through his hair. Looking straight into his gorgeous brown eyes, she felt the chattering children and the music fade away and had to fight an enormous wave of emotion just to get her next words out. Clutching the box containing the ring to her heart for a moment, she took his fingers.

'Ana, what is it?' he whispered. She almost giggled at the concern and confusion on his face, but Ines was encouraging her, nodding for her to continue, as they had planned when they'd chosen the ring for him.

'Being your friend was wonderful,' she said. 'Being your girlfriend is even more so. But, Gabriel, I want more than anything to be your wife.' She opened the box up slowly and swallowed a last flurry of nerves as an audible gasp travelled around the room. 'I love you. Will you be my husband? Will you marry me?'

Gabriel's eyebrows shot to his hairline. He seemed nearly as taken aback as everyone else, and he just stared at the ring for what felt like for ever. Then finally, in a soft voice, he said, 'Yes.'

He stood up, letting her push the ring onto his finger, a grin breaking out on his face. 'Yes!' he exclaimed loudly, lifting her clean from her chair and spinning her around. Pandemonium broke out among the children as they laughed and Gabriel kissed her. Everyone was clapping and cheering, no-one louder than Javi, and she even caught Ines crying softly as she leaned into Pedro's shoulder.

'You're crazy, but I am in love with you,' Gabriel whispered, just as a giant fuzzy watermelon jumped up for one more group kiss. This time Ana didn't push him off. There was enough love here for everyone, however they wanted to show it.

* * * * *

*Look out for the next story in the
Buenos Aires Docs quartet*

Secretly Dating the Baby Doc
by JC Harroway

*And if you enjoyed this story, check out
these other great reads from Becky Wicks*

Melting the Surgeon's Heart
Finding Forever with the Single Dad
South African Escape to Heal Her

All available now!

HARLEQUIN
Reader Service

Enjoyed your book?

Try the perfect subscription for Romance readers and get more great books like this delivered right to your door.

See why over 10+ million readers have tried Harlequin Reader Service.

Start with a Free Welcome Collection with free books and a gift—valued over $20.

Choose any series in print or ebook. See website for details and order today:

TryReaderService.com/subscriptions